COLD STEAL

COLD STEAL

A LEONIDAS WITHERALL MYSTERY

Phoebe Atwood Taylor

WRITING AS ALICE TILTON

A FOUL PLAY PRESS BOOK

THE COUNTRYMAN PRESS, WOODSTOCK, VERMONT

This edition published in 1980 by Foul Play Press, a division of The Countryman Press, Woodstock, Vermont 05091, distributed by The Independent Publishers Group, 14 Vanderventer Avenue, Port Washington, New York 11050.

ISBN 0-914378-54-6
Printed in the United States of America

For
K. B.

COLD STEAL

CHAPTER I

A TIDAL WAVE of gray flannel dressing gown streamed out behind Miss Chard as she bolted like a bewildered mouse across the vestibule platforms from Car Ten into Car Nine.

Once inside, she huddled against the cold metal of the parlor car wall, her eyes glued to the door, and her ears strained for the sound of footsteps that never came. While mile after mile of snow-spotted fields, drab and leaden in the chill New England dawn, rushed past the corridor windows, she stood there watching and listening and trembling, and clutching at the brown paper package in her dressing gown pocket.

In the face of her apparently overpowering fear, the fact that she could still remember her immediate objective stood out as a tribute to her tenacity. That she could actually force her felt-slippered feet to start moving on down the narrow corridor was an achievement, a positive triumph of will power and strength of mind.

Only her strong will, Miss Chard thought as she stopped in front of the water cooler, accounted for her being alive and on the train. Her body was simply an innocent and panic-stricken bystander that since seven o'clock the previous evening had been shoved hither and yon through a suddenly tumultuous and chaotic world.

Her dangling gray braid bobbed from side to side at the recollection of the last twelve hours, of those Dalton policemen and their guns, the sirens screeching, and then the airplane trip to New York. Then, practically before she got the cotton out of her ears and the gum taste out of her mouth, she was on this train and going back home again. And throughout it all there hadn't been a single moment when Miss Chard was not terrified to the core.

She still was.

But now she had only this final gesture to make before turning Leslie Horn over to her aunt. Once Leslie Horn was placed, figuratively speaking, in the arms of Medora Winthrop, Miss Chard's nightmare would be over.

Resolutely, she drew from her pocket the brown paper package of whose contents she stood in such mortal fear. Before Leslie Horn waked up, that package had to be thrown away, a task made unbelievably formidable by the tightly fitting Pullman windows that remained unmoved in response to her tuggings. She had considered disposing of the package by way of an open vestibule door, but to open one seemed to her dangerous, and besides, the sign said that passengers mustn't.

Miss Chard peered beyond into Car Nine and its still slumbering occupants, and then over her shoulder in the direction of Car Ten.

Then, hastily, she buried the brown paper package deep down out of sight in the bottom of the receptacle for used drinking cups, at the base of the water cooler. For good measure, she yanked a handful of clean cups from the wall container and strewed them on the top layer, above the package.

"There!" Miss Chard whispered. "There!"

Her feeling of relief at completing her little mission, as she turned from the water cooler, gave way to a gasp of acute dismay.

Framed in the doorway of Drawing Room A, and observing her interestedly, stood an elderly man with a small pointed beard.

He looked like Shakespeare. He looked so much like Shakespeare that it seemed as if some library bust or engraved frontispiece had come suddenly to life.

"I hope," Leonidas Witherall began courteously, "that I didn't frighten—"

But Miss Chard was already in flight.

Leonidas Witherall sighed in annoyance as the gray dressing gown streamed past him up the narrow corridor and out of the car.

He didn't mind the woman's gasp. A gasp was not at all an unusual reaction from someone beholding him for the first time. He was thoroughly accustomed to being gasped at and gaped at and stared at. Dozens of people did so daily, and fully half of them asked excitedly if anyone had ever told him that he looked like Shakespeare. Occasionally some ardent Shakespeare lover went so far as to prod him to see if he was real.

All that was routine, and Leonidas accepted it. But a flight was different. He resented having mousy women stampede at the sight of him, as if he were a monster. This was the third fugitive within a month, and every last one had been a grayish, mousy woman who scuttled.

Leonidas stepped across the corridor to survey the dreary, snow-heaped landscape flashing by.

He was amazed and a little discouraged at the number of mousy women who seemed constantly traveling. On the trip around the world which he was just concluding, he had been haunted from the start by throngs of mousy women. Wherever he went, he was confronted by mousy women taking snapshots, or buying wicker baskets and never-ending strings of beads, or writing the dates and dimensions of things in little black notebooks.

They worried about fleas, and crawling insects, and where the lettuce came from. They lost trunks, and that worried them. They lost pocketbooks, and that worried them more. And only those things they worried about were allowed to creep into their conversation. But he could forgive their dullness, Leonidas thought. He could even forgive this new habit of stampeding at the sight of him, if they weren't all so uncompromisingly plain and mousy.

Leonidas swung his pince-nez from their broad black ribbon.

Perhaps it was all his fault for not outgrowing the E. Phillips Oppenheim tradition, but he had never entirely been able to banish a conviction that on every train or every ship there should be at least one intensely beautiful woman, who, furthermore, should be guarding a pouch stuffed with stolen emeralds. Lacking emeralds, the beautiful woman should have crammed beneath her girdle a handful of secret treaties, or pilfered designs for superdreadnoughts, or anyway a plan for Der Tag.

But if such exciting creatures existed, they always avoided the conveyances on which Leonidas traveled. Very likely the throngs of mousy women scared them off, which he considered a great pity.

Swinging his pince-nez, he watched more fields rush past. The snow became increasingly deeper as they neared Boston, and the sky was gloomy and overcast.

"Not an inspiring sight."

Leonidas turned around. Busy with his bitter thoughts concerning mousy women, he hadn't noticed the young man in the blue suit who had emerged from Car Nine, and was standing almost at his elbow.

"Not— My God, you *do* look like Shakespeare, don't you?"

"So," Leonidas said, "I have been told."

He started to move along up the corridor, but the young man, apparently entranced by his discovery, continued to block the way and stare at him raptly.

"I say, when I was a youngster, I went to Meredith's Academy, and there was a professor in the upper school they used to call Bill Shakespeare. I've forgotten his real name. No one ever called him by it, anyway. Aren't you him?"

"Were you graduated from Meredith's?" Leonidas asked gently.

"No, I went on to Dumbert," the young man said.

Leonidas nodded. "I felt sure that if you had come under my jurisdiction in the English Department, you would not ask me if I wasn't him. Actually, I am he."

A more sensitive ear would have caught the faint

implication of a snub, but the young man only laughed.

"Well, you know Dumbert. Just a bunch of illiterates. We went in more for football and stuff. I can't spell, either— Say, will you look out at those drifts? The porter said Boston got two feet of snow yesterday, and there's supposed to be a cold wave coming, too. New England in March! Honestly, did you ever see anything drearier than those fields in this light? Doesn't it depress you?"

There was something infectious about the young man's buoyant vigor, and Leonidas took off his pince-nez and gave up trying to remain aloof.

"Ordinarily," he said, "I should avert my eyes. But this morning, I find the landscape rather stimulating."

"What? Now you don't mean," the young man waved a hand toward the window, "that—that Godforsaken vista gives you any lift?"

"It does. You see, I'm going home. And it's the first time in years I've had a home to go to." Leonidas, who had no intention of doing anything of the kind, suddenly found to his surprise that he was unburdening himself to this chatty young fellow. "A brand new house, built just for me. A small white house with green blinds. And I've never seen it."

"How come?" the young man asked interestedly as he lighted a cigarette. "If I ever built me a house, I'd sit and watch every nail get driven, and stick my fingers in the concrete, and play with the shavings—why, that's half the fun of building a house!"

"I suppose so," Leonidas said. "But I was in a hurry to see the world once more while there was still some world left to see, and the tangle of my uncle's estate wasn't settled enough for me to spend more money before I went. Then when I heard the estate was settled, I cabled my friends to get busy—"

"You let your friends build you a house while you were away? It's fantastic!" the young man said. "It's incredible!"

Leonidas shook his head. "Not really. I had the land, and the plans. In fact, I had the plans long before I had the land, or the money to build a house with."

"Sort of a dream house, huh?"

"In a way," Leonidas said. "I've never seen it, but I know just how it's going to look, and how the staircase curves, and where each book will go. And— What did you say?"

"I choked. Just a stray New Haven cinder. Well, sir, I think you had courage to let other people build your dream house— My God, it's six-thirty, and I promised to wake Mike at six! I've got to rush. Good luck to you in your new house!"

Leonidas watched his departure with amusement. He didn't for a moment believe that there was anyone named Mike who had to be awakened. The young man had invented him as an excuse to escape hearing further details about the new house. It served him right, Leonidas thought, for being so chatty with strangers.

Putting on his pince-nez, he turned back to the window. In an hour he would be in the South Station, and in another hour he would be home. Once settled, he would start the new Lieutenant Haseltine book, for which his publishers clamored. He never intended to continue the Haseltine series now that he had an income again, but the Haseltine habit proved too strong to break. He had written three Haseltine books a year for so many years that he automatically wrote about the daring lieutenant whether he meant to or not.

He wondered what his friends would say if they knew he was the author of the Haseltine books. He wondered what the mousy women would make of that intrepid officer.

Chuckling at the thought, he started up the corridor. A cup of coffee in the club car would help while away the time.

He stopped suddenly in front of the water cooler, and stared reflectively at the "Out of Order" sign dangling from the faucet lever.

That, he reflected, was odd. It hadn't been out of order when the mousy woman was getting her drink a few minutes before.

Then it occurred to him that he had not actually seen her either getting the drink or in the act of drinking. He had taken that for granted. As a matter of fact, the woman had just been sort of fumbling around.

And the top layer of discarded cups was curiously dry and unsullied.

Why, Leonidas wondered, would the mousy woman wastefully strew dry cups around? Pique, possibly. Perhaps the mousy woman was wasting the Pullman Company's cups in a spirit of revenge.

"A mouse," Leonidas murmured. "A mouse, gnawing at a mountain. M'yes."

But if the woman was being vindictive, why hadn't she made a clean sweep? There were still plenty of cups left up in the wall container.

The pince-nez described a series of small circles while Leonidas swung them and pondered.

Now that he considered the situation, that gasp had been more in the nature of a guilty start than an exclamation of amazement at his appearance. Perhaps his looking and not his looks had prompted that gasp and that flight.

Leonidas fixed his attention on the top layer of paper cups. When you took the trouble to camouflage the top of anything, you usually wished to hide what was at the bottom. At Meredith's, he had learned to

be suspicious of unduly neat top layers in his weekly
inspection of dormitory bureau drawers. A brisk fish-
ing invariably brought to light any number of strange
and illicit objects, like those famous stink bombs of
Hartley Minor's.

Leaning forward, Leonidas fished.

With a gleam in his blue eyes, he extricated Miss
Chard's brown paper package.

Obviously, by the feel of it, the package contained
neither stolen emeralds nor a handful of secret treaties.
But if the contents included what Leonidas guessed
they did, then he had erred in his judgments concerning the activities of mousy women who traveled. He
had underestimated them, definitely.

Back inside his drawing room, Leonidas discovered
that he had guessed correctly. Under the brown paper
wrapping there was a gun, a small but sinister-looking
revolver. And, in addition to the gun, there was also
a pair of sleek and shining handcuffs.

After gazing at them for a critical moment, Leonidas
replaced the wrapping, tied up the package, and returned it to its former hiding place at the base of the
water cooler. Guns and handcuffs played no part in
his life. He had no use for them, nor any desire to
become involved in difficult explanations, should anyone in authority demand them and start asking questions.

Besides, he felt there was more chance of his curiosity being satisfied by replacing the package, and waiting to see what would happen next.

For he was positive that the mousy woman would return. From his infinite experience with them, he knew that mousy women made a fetish of Making Sure. He had seen them open pocketbooks twenty times in five minutes to make sure that their tickets were safe. On train platforms, in customs sheds, on wharves, he had watched mousy women constantly unlocking suitcases and pawing through trunks to make sure that their possessions were where they had been put.

Because she had been observed, this mousy woman with the braid would certainly come back and check up on her brown paper package, the minute the coast was clear. She would employ the interval by telling herself reassuringly that the man who looked like Shakespeare had not seen a thing, and that he would have made some other comment if he had. But she would never be able to restrain herself from coming back and making sure. Sooner or later, she would return.

Leonidas wedged his drawing room door open to a thin crack, and sat down to await developments. It exasperated him somewhat to think that at the end of his journey, with only three-quarters of an hour to go, something mildly akin to adventure should at last turn up.

The chatty young man walked rather hurriedly past the door. He was followed by a porter, and a querulous man in magenta pajamas, who was complaining bitterly that he hadn't slept a wink.

They, however, all came from Car Nine, and the mousy woman ought to be coming the other way, from Car Ten.

The rush and roar of a passing train drowned out all other sounds, and in the flickering slits of light as the cars slatted past, Leonidas nearly missed the flash of gray past his door. For a puzzled moment, he wondered if he had imagined it.

A series of clinks as something metallic dropped on the corridor floor brought him to his feet.

He had known, Leonidas told himself with satisfaction, that she would come back. She was the type.

But in the doorway, he stopped short.

It was not the mousy woman who knelt on her hands and knees on the floor. It was a strikingly beautiful girl in a gray suit who peered up at him, and smiled disarmingly.

"You've dropped something?" Leonidas inquired.

"Practically everything," the girl said. "A cigarette case, and a lighter, and a lipstick, and— Oh, here's the case. Is that the lipstick in that crack by you?"

Obligingly, Leonidas got down on all fours and hunted in the crack.

"Here's the lighter," the girl said. "I've found the lighter. Oh, damn, I *hate* losing that lipstick! It's my pet lipstick. I suppose it's rolled around and got stuck under— Oh, porter! Do you see my lipstick anywhere?"

The porter joined their crablike scramble around the narrow corridor, a sight which enchanted the chatty young man when he returned once again to Car Nine.

"Playing leapfrog?" he asked genially. "Can anyone join? Oh, you've lost something. I see. Well, if the lady in gray will rise and give me her place, old Hawkeye will find it. Move over, Shakespeare."

Another porter co-operated, and so did the train conductor and the Pullman conductor. But it was Leonidas who eventually found the lipstick at the far end of the corridor, imbedded under the linoleum by the entrance door.

"You're wonderful!" the girl said. "You've all been simply marvelous, and I can't begin to tell you all how grateful I am! Really, you—"

Long before she finished her speech of thanks, the group was glowing with pleasure and good fellowship, and the feeling that they had all been of tremendous service in an undertaking of major importance.

All, that is, except Leonidas.

Although he glowed outwardly with the rest, he found himself wishing that the girl wouldn't lay it on so thickly with her trowel. To be sure, none of the others noticed. Whether it was the girl's voice that charmed them, or her face, or her figure, or her soft red curls, the fact remained that the group was charmed. Not even the chatty young man thought to ask how that lipstick possibly could have imbedded itself in such a way that the blades of two pocketknives were necessary to pry it out.

Leonidas's admiration for the girl mounted. By sheer force of personal magnetism, she had made two porters, two conductors, and the chatty young man feel that a lipstick so imbedded was an ordinary, commonplace occurrence. Any one of them would have been shocked at the suggestion that the lipstick was planted. They would probably challenge to a duel anyone who told them they had been bamboozled.

Really, Leonidas thought, the girl apparently lacked only one qualification of an E. Phillips Oppenheim heroine. She had no accent.

For, while the men were scrambling on the floor, the girl had removed the brown paper package from the base of the water cooler.

Calmly and unhurriedly, with her back toward the cooler, she had fished out the package and popped it into her smart black suède pocketbook. And, throughout the operation, she had maintained a delightful and diverting conversation. She spurred the men on to greater efforts. She described the barber-pole striping of the lipstick's case. She told how much she paid for it. She told them the flavor.

No one but Leonidas had noticed what went on as she chatted. There was no reason why they should have noticed. The idea of hunting a lipstick had been firmly planted in their minds, and they hunted a lipstick to the exclusion of everything else. A brown paper package containing a gun and a pair of handcuffs had never been suggested to them, while Leonidas had the advantage of knowing about it.

"Simply marvelous, all of you," the girl concluded. "And—oh, while I think of it, conductor, here are the checks. You won't disturb my aunt, will you? I left a notice on the door. She wants to sleep as late as the law allows. Thanks, loads. Now," she went on briskly, "I must get along and find the rest of my family. Car Five's to the rear, isn't it? Good-by, everybody, and thank you again, Shakespeare!"

Her parting smile to Leonidas made him wonder if she knew that he knew. He was sure that she guessed.

He wanted to follow the girl. He yearned to follow her and get to the root of this tantalizing little episode. He had every opportunity to follow her, for the other men, including the chatty young man, had gone their respective ways. But something held him there in the doorway of his drawing room, and after a minute or two he went inside and closed the door firmly behind him.

Tantalizing or not, he told himself, it was none of his business, and this was no time for him to indulge any quixotic impulses. He was twenty-one minutes from the South Station, an hour and twenty-one minutes from the new house. If this had only happened earlier, he would have plunged with enthusiasm into the solution of a puzzle that cried for a solution. But right now, he was going home.

It disturbed him, as he gathered his things together, to find that he couldn't keep the mousy woman out of his thoughts. But he kept seeing that gray braid and hearing that gasp.

The facts were so simple. A package was put somewhere, and then taken out. But if the mousy woman were the girl's aunt, she was wide awake enough when he saw her. Why should she now wish to sleep as long as the law allowed? If the aunt and the girl were together, why should the aunt hide the package, and the girl retrieve it?

That line of thought reduced everything to an absurdity, so Leonidas started in from another angle.

How on earth had the girl known that the package was there? And why had she laid such elaborate plans to get it? First she had planted that lipstick, and then she had deliberately dropped things from her pocket-book. The sound of them falling was negligible in comparison with all the train noises, but it would be sufficient to lure anyone who might be lurking around and listening. Had no one appeared, she could have taken the package and departed, secure in the knowledge that she hadn't been observed. If anyone turned up, she had the stage set to instigate the lipstick hunt. During that bit of manufactured distraction, she could get her package anyway.

It was the old magician's trick. Plant something in the left hand to catch the audience's eye, and let the right hand do what it would. It had worked out beautifully. It had been beautifully planned. There was a professional gloss to the whole incident that had been entirely lacking in the episode of the mousy woman.

Where was that woman? Why hadn't she returned? Where had she gone? What happened to her?

Leonidas locked a pigskin case, pushed it aside, and got up.

He could sit till doomsday and improvise on the theme of the mousy woman, but a two-minute investigation would probably solve everything.

Rapidly, he walked through to Car Ten.

He was far too preoccupied and in far too much of a hurry to notice that the chatty young man suddenly cut short his conversation with a porter in the aisle of Car Nine, and sauntered slowly after him.

Inside Car Ten, Leonidas paused. The girl had pointed toward it when she gave her checks to the conductor, and since there were only coaches ahead, it was obviously the car from which she'd come. Her mention of putting a notice on the door indicated that she had occupied a drawing room.

And from the doorknob of Drawing Room B hung a "Do NOT Disturb" card.

It was utterly foolish of him, Leonidas thought, to jump to the conclusion that the mousy woman and the aunt referred to by the girl should be the same person. He hadn't a whiff of evidence to suspect that the mousy woman might be drugged, slugged, or otherwise in distress within this drawing room. He was letting himself be carried away by the Oppenheim tradition and by his own elastic imagination.

If he ignored the sign and pounded until he aroused some sleeping passenger, he would feel like an unqualified imbecile. If, on the other hand, he didn't discover what had become of the mousy woman, she and her braid would haunt him to the end of his days.

Leonidas raised his hand.

The door promptly swung open at his knock, apparently of its own accord. No one was holding it. It swayed back and forth with the motion of the train.

Without entering, Leonidas peered inside.

The shades were drawn. The berths were pulled apart. The blankets were heaped in a pile. There was no sign of the mousy woman, or of any luggage, or of anything else.

In short, Drawing Room B of Car Ten was vacant.

Leonidas sighed. Once more the Oppenheim tradition had let him down. No lifeless bodies, no beautiful girl, no intrigue, no emeralds, not even a crumpled paper on the floor.

Keenly disappointed, feeling even a twinge of resentment, Leonidas started to turn away. He grabbed at the door jamb as the train lurched, and while he steadied himself, something rolled across the drawing room floor and hit against his shoe.

Even with the shades down, there was no mistaking the barber-pole stripes of that lipstick! It was the girls' lipstick, the one they had hunted for.

This was her drawing room, and she had returned to it!

Leonidas stepped inside and snapped on the lights.

He heard the door slam suddenly, and the click of its bolt in the lock. He knew someone was behind him. He knew instinctively that he should duck.

But he couldn't duck. He couldn't move. His attention was riveted to the pile of blankets, and the body hidden beneath them. He assumed there was a body. All he could see was a hand.

When he did manage to swing around, it was too late.

The butt of a revolver cracked against the side of his head, and sent him sprawling.

The train lurched as he fell, and a metal seat leg seemed to rise and meet him in mid-air. In the split second before he achieved complete oblivion, Leonidas had one last coherent thought.

He was less dazed by the crack than the fact that the mousy woman was the cracker.

CHAPTER II

LEONIDAS OPENED his eyes, blinked them, and then closed them firmly.

He had reason to believe that he was conscious. There were certain very definite indications that he had come to. He was aware of a fretful throbbing in his head. He could wiggle his toes. He could hear train sounds and the subdued voices of people talking.

On the other hand, certain points confused him.

There was, for example, no train motion. He was not in the drawing room. He was lolling on a green plush Pullman seat surrounded by a cluster of egglike faces, all wearing interested stares.

Leonidas opened his eyes again and stared back.

There was no mousy woman among them, no beautiful girl, and the only limpid body in the vicinity appeared to be his own.

"Take it easy, Shakespeare. You're okay." The chatty young man in the blue suit leaned over him and spoke in friendly, reassuring tones, as though Leonidas

were a small, dull cousin. "You'll be perfectly all
right if you take it easy. It's nothing serious. You just
gave yourself a nasty crack over the head."

"I did not!" Leonidas told him indignantly.

"What?"

"I said, I did not. I did nothing of the kind! D'you
think that *I'm* responsible for—"

"There, there!" said the young man. "Calm down!
You didn't crack yourself, you sustained a bump, if
you like that better. My God, even in this state, you
can stickle for unity, emphasis, and coherence! But
you're all right, Shakespeare. The doctor saw you, and
he said it was nothing compared to the man—"

A conductor, one of the two who had aided in the
lipstick search, edged his way into the circle.

"The ambulance'll be ready for him in a few minutes, Mr. Dow."

Leonidas sat up and affixed his pince-nez, which
were miraculously unscathed and intact.

"Er—just what ambulance will be ready for whom?"

"The one that Mr. Dow," the conductor pointed to
the chatty young man, "ordered for you. It'll be here
in a couple minutes."

"If," Leonidas said, "if, by any stretch of the imagination, you mean that an ambulance has been ordered
and is ready for me, please dismiss it promptly. Where
is the body?"

"Body?" Mr. Dow and the rest surveyed Leonidas with benign tolerance.

"Body," Leonidas said. "Where is it?"

"Oh, I get you," Mr. Dow said. "What a quaint way of putting it! Your body is in the South Station. You've been out since before Back Bay, because I saw you start from your drawing room back there, and you just turned up a minute ago."

"Indeed," Leonidas said. "Indeed! And what is the consensus concerning the interval?"

"Huh?" said the conductor. "What's that?"

Leonidas tried again.

"What is popularly assumed to be the reason for my —er—my out?"

Under the circumstances, he thought it wiser to ask than to volunteer his own impressions. The little group surrounding him were realists. They knew he had been knocked out, and they could see the bump which he was beginning to feel on the side of his head. To these people, he was an elderly bearded man who had just come to, a dazed, confused creature who required an ambulance.

A statement of simple truths was out of the question.

This was not the time to tell the conductor and the young man named Dow that the lipstick hunt at which they assisted was actually an interlude of intrigue, during which a beautiful girl swiped a package containing a gun and a pair of handcuffs from the base of a water cooler, where it had been thrust by a mousy frightened woman with a braid. This was not the time to mention cracks from revolver butts, or inert bodies under blankets.

Such a recital would inspire more than an ambulance. Swayed by only the most humane motives, Leonidas thought, they would whisk him at once into a strait jacket.

But as he listened to Mr. Dow's chatty explanation of what knocked him out, he began to regret his caution.

For Mr. Dow said it was a snow plow.

"That's what gave you the bump, Shakespeare. Just a snow plow."

Leonidas made a thwarted sound in the back of his throat.

"That is," Mr. Dow continued, "it was basically a snow plow. Our train almost bumped it, or we almost were bumped by it—that part is one of those moot points. Anyway, brakes got put on hard, and a bump ensued, and it apparently pitched you head first into the drawing room beyond here. The door must have been unlatched, and in you flew with the greatest of ease, and then apparently the door slammed shut behind you. But you're nowhere near as badly off as a fellow in Car Seven. They're afraid his skull's fractured, and the doctor's rushed him off to the hospital. And you should see the lady with the goose eggs in Car Ten."

Leonidas sighed, and took off his pince-nez. To think that he had balked at telling this group a simple incident involving a mousy woman and a brown paper package, and the group retaliated with a yarn about snow plows and goose eggs!

"No, Mr. Dow," Leonidas said politely. "No. I can't take the goose eggs, even from an old Meredith boy."

"That's a fact, Shakespeare," the young man assured him. "Two dozen goose eggs. She got 'em in New York, and was taking 'em home to her children to color for Easter. Car Ten's a vast omelet."

The group agreed that Car Ten was a mess.

"Er—tell me," Leonidas interrupted their descriptive efforts, "how did I come to light, Mr. Dow?"

"I found you just now. The drawing room door popped open as we pulled out of Back Bay. I happened to be going by, and spotted you, or you'd be there yet. Now, Shakespeare, if you—"

"One moment," Leonidas said. "I was on the floor of the empty drawing room? Er—alone?"

"That's right," the conductor said. "That girl we

hunted the lipstick for—remember her? It was her drawing room. She and her aunt had it."

His tone implied that it was pretty fortunate of Leonidas to have picked that particular drawing room for his accident.

"M'yes," Leonidas said. "The aunt who was going to sleep as long as the law allowed? That aunt? Er—where were they when I pitched in headlong?"

"The aunt changed her mind all of a sudden," the conductor explained. "Decided all of a sudden she wanted to get off at Back Bay, and then hurry across and catch a Carnavon local out of Trinity Place Station. The girl asked me how they could make it, so I told 'em to go up to the coach ahead, so they wouldn't lose time waiting for the porter here to take bags out. See?"

"Frankly," Leonidas said, "no."

"Why, they'd left the drawing room, see? The girl hunted me up just after we stopped for the plow, and asked me how they could get off quick at Back Bay, because her aunt changed her mind all of a sudden and decided she wanted to catch a Carnavon local, see? So I took 'em both to the coach—"

"To sum it all up, Shakespeare," Mr. Dow said, "Beautiful and her aunt had beaten it before you dropped in. Does it really matter? I mean, do you really care? Because I told the doctor I'd take you home in cotton wool, and call your family physician, and I see the wheel chair's waiting for you out on the platform—that means the ambulance's ready, doesn't it, conductor?"

"That's right. But he's got to see our other doctor," the conductor said, "and Mr. Clancy, and Mr. Delaney, and Mr. O'Brien and the rest. They're going through getting names of anyone that got hurt—"

"Whyn't you whip along and bring 'em in here?" Mr. Dow suggested. "Then we can get the red tape over with, and get poor Mr. Witherall home. Okay? And maybe a couple of you," he appealed to the surrounding group, "would see to his bags and coat and stuff, and sort of get 'em collected? Drawing Room A in Car Ten. Get some porters for the bags, and bring his coat and hat here. I'll stay here with him."

The group dispersed.

"There," Mr. Dow said. "Now we're making progress. A brief trundle in a wheel chair, and a cosy dash in the ambulance, and you'll be home in Dalton in no time, Mr. Witherall—"

"How did you know I lived in Dalton?" Leonidas asked.

Mr. Dow smiled his infectious smile.

"I picked your pocket while you were in no condition to protest," he said. "I pulled out your wallet, and learned you were Leonidas Witherall, Forty Birch Hill Road, Dalton Centre. I say, sir, I hope you don't think I've been too fresh, mixing myself up in this, and calling you Shakespeare, and all. But honestly, I never knew you to be called anything but Bill Shakespeare!"

"I'm resigned to that. But, Mr. Dow, I should—"

"And I really was worried about you at first," Mr. Dow went on earnestly. "You looked awful. Then when that doctor said you'd be all right—"

"What doctor?"

"The one that looked at you. He went off with the fellow from Car Seven they thought had the fractured skull. When he said you'd be all right, I wondered if it wouldn't be better—well, you'd told me how you looked forward to seeing your house, and I thought you'd rather continue on home than be shunted off to a relief station."

"Indeed, yes. But I feel that—"

But Mr. Dow was already talking again. The fellow seemed determined not to let Leonidas finish a sentence, and Leonidas personally didn't feel equal to outshouting him.

"I knew there was no one to meet you, sir, so I just up and took charge. Carpe diem, as they used to say at Meredith's— Do you feel any worse, sir?"

"No," Leonidas said, "but I should—"

"Really? You're sure you don't feel any worse, sir?

I thought you looked sort of anguished, just then. You looked funny. You're probably sore all over, aren't you? But I do hope," Mr. Dow rattled on, giving Leonidas no opportunity to say a word, "that you're not sore with me, sir. I really did my best to— Look, here comes the conductor with a lot of red-faced men. If you'll just maintain that anguished expression while they ask questions, you might stand to make some money out of this little accident."

During the interval that followed, Leonidas rather absent-mindedly allowed himself to be thumped and poked and prodded by a brusque little doctor who said there was nothing whatever the matter with Mr. Witherall except a bump on the head, and he'd feel right as rain in a few hours, if only he kept still and didn't try to move a brick house. Everyone, including Mr. Dow, seemed to think that was a splendid bit of news, and everyone told Leonidas that he was a very lucky man.

They were right, Leonidas decided as he gave his name and address to all the red-faced men. He was a lucky man. He was also something of a fool.

For Leonidas had been doing some rapid thinking.

He had left Southampton on the day he intended, but he had left on a different and faster boat, thereby arriving in New York twenty-four hours earlier than anyone expected. His friends had not been told of the change. And because none of them knew he was coming, no one was going to meet him at the station.

But only Leonidas knew that.

As far as anyone else was concerned, or as far as any passenger on this train knew, he might be awaiting a rousing municipal welcome, with brass bands and confetti streamers, and delegations of distinguished citizens bearing keys to the city.

How had the young, voluble Mr. Dow known otherwise?

But he had. Very definitely and distinctly, Mr. Dow had said, "I knew there was no one to meet you, so I took charge."

The largest of the red-faced men gave Leonidas a card.

"Thank you, Mr. Witherall. Someone will call on you tomorrow. You've been far more co-operative than some of the passengers who—er—were more fortunate. Is that his coat? Let me help you with your coat, Mr. Witherall. There, sir! There you are!"

Once over the first dizziness of standing up, Leonidas felt entirely capable of walking under his own power. Brushing aside someone's suggestion that he should be carried, he started down the car aisle.

In front of Drawing Room B, he paused and smiled at the red-faced men.

"When I fell in here, I had a small silver pencil in

my hand," he said. "D'you suppose one of you might find it for me? I shouldn't bother you, but it was given me by my old friend the Maharajah, and I cherish it highly."

Leonidas always felt that if one had to lie, one might as well do it with a flourish.

"Certainly, Mr. Witherall! Of course, of course!"

The nearest red-faced man thrust open the drawing room door with such force that an attendant, who had already started cleaning, was frightened out of his wits.

While everyone hunted for the mythical pencil, Leonidas looked the room over very thoroughly.

Obviously the place had not been hastily spruced up for his, or anyone else's, inspection. The cleaner was simply going about his ordinary work. The gray blankets were there, neatly folded, but there certainly was no body, nor any trace of one.

Leonidas hadn't really expected to find any. But he had proved to his own satisfaction that if there was any conspiracy, it was not one in which the conductor, or the porter, or the red-faced officials played any part. To them, everything concerned with the drawing room was in order, and they were perfectly willing to enter it, or to have him enter. Besides, if they had wanted him out of the way, they easily could have rushed him off to a hospital for observation. But they had made no effort to do anything of the kind. They had been as solicitous and kind as anyone could wish.

Swinging his pince-nez, Leonidas considered the blue serge shoulders of Mr. Dow.

Very definitely, things were boiling down to that chatty young man.

"Suppose," Leonidas said, "that when the pencil is found, it is sent to me? I'm sure that you gentlemen have other things to do—"

"Sure, Mr. Witherall. You want to get along home. Of course. We'll find the Maharajah's pencil and get it to you. Clancy, you go ahead and help Mr. Witherall with the steps."

As he was trundled along the station platform in the waiting wheel chair, with Clancy and Dow and a bevy of laden porters swarming around him, Leonidas began to feel somewhat like a Maharajah, himself. A Maharajah in a box on an elephant. He tried to remember the proper term.

"Howdah," he said at last. "Howdah!"

The porter pushing the wheel chair looked vaguely disturbed.

"Yes, suh. I'm okay. You okay, suh?"

"A howdah is a type of litter—er—let it pass."

The fine points of a howdah, Leonidas decided after noting the porter's expression, were better left unthrashed.

Besides, he had before him the problem of young Mr. Dow, and what to do about him.

An impartial observer would sum up Mr. Dow as a right-living, right-thinking, good-looking young man, probably a devoted son, from the way he hovered anxiously around the wheel chair.

But that habit of hovering was one of the things which Leonidas did not like about young Mr. Dow. He could find no fault with the actual quality of the hovering. It was deft and amiable and ingratiating. Mr. Dow was not a one to push. What troubled Leonidas was so much hovering.

Mr. Dow had been hovering out in the corridor just after the mousy woman fled. He was hovering around before the girl came. Leonidas remembered his passing by the door crack. He turned up for the lipstick hunt. He must have been hovering somewhere in the vicinity if he saw Leonidas leave his drawing room, and he must have been hovering somewhere else to have found Leonidas. He had hovered over and cut short the conductor's explanations of why the girl and her aunt had left the drawing room.

And the way that young Mr. Dow hovered around him, Leonidas thought, was phenomenal. An old Meredith boy, someone whom Leonidas had known personally, might have taken such an interest. But this Dow, by his own confession, went to Dumbert's.

And the average Dumbert product considered it a sign of weakness to display even the commoner courtesies to anyone connected with Meredith's.

Then, of course, there was Mr. Dow's glib prattle, which more than once had been very forced indeed.

But you couldn't condemn a man for hovering. You couldn't dismiss Mr. Dow as a base villain, and say that somehow he must be involved in a plot with the mousy woman and the girl, just because he happened to be near the spot.

Only one definite slip had been made, and that was Mr. Dow's unguarded and inexplicable remark about there being no one to meet Leonidas at the station. That could be charitably termed a casual assumption on the part of Mr. Dow. On the other hand, it could also indicate that Mr. Dow had been engaging himself in energetic research concerning the plans and affairs of Leonidas Witherall.

And then there was the ambulance angle.

Leonidas had barely started to consider what sort of foul play might be indicated by this waiting ambulance, when Clancy walked over to the wheel chair.

"You feel all right, Mr. Witherall?"

Leonidas assured Clancy that he felt fine.

"You look worried, sort of. Say, Mr. Witherall, this young fellow Dow, he says he lives in Dalton, and he's going along with you. But look, I'd be glad to get someone else, if you'd tell me who to call. Or a nurse. There won't be a nurse with the ambulance, because he had to call a private one, on account of it having to go out of the city. But if you'd like a nurse, I'll get one."

Leonidas promptly seized his opportunity.

"Really, Mr. Clancy, I don't need a nurse. Or an ambulance. I've no intention of going home in any ambulance. I vetoed that idea a long while ago."

Young Mr. Dow, who had been listening, nodded his head vigorously.

"I agree with you. I don't think you need an ambulance, either. But the doctor said you ought to be quiet, and a cab will jounce—"

"I got it," Clancy said. "I got it! Get one of Sammy's limousines. Over there." He pointed to the Car Hire sign. "Tell Sammy it's for me. That all right with you, Mr. Witherall? It's on the house, anyway. Ask Sammy for Carl, Mr. Dow, and be sure and tell him it's me that wants him."

"I think," Leonidas said, "that a cab will do."

"Sure, it'll do, but one of Sammy's cars'll be better. We'll wait here for Dow. You know, Mr. Witherall, I never thought till Dow suggested it that maybe you wouldn't like going off with a stranger like this. I think, myself, Dow's a nice fellow and all right. But like he said to me, as far as you know, he might be kidnaping

you, or after your money, or something. I just wanted
to say, you'll be okay with one of Sammy's cars, and
Carl. I know 'em both. Carl's a fine driver."

"What on earth," Leonidas asked, "made Mr. Dow
feel that I needed to be reassured about him, I wonder? What reason have I to suspect Mr. Dow of
ulterior motives?"

Clancy looked embarrassed.

"Well, like he said, you're an—er—older man, like
—not that plenty of younger men wouldn't be still out
with a bump like yours, Mr. Witherall! Dow just
thought, you were upset—uh—he's waving to us. We'll
go out the other entrance. I'll push the chair."

Leonidas was assisted into the black limousine at
the curb, and in spite of his protests, Clancy wrapped
a robe around his knees.

"There! What about trunks? Oh, they been sent
express. How about bags? How many? Twelve pieces,
a cane and a camera. Right? Okay, Mr. Witherall.
Now, Carl, listen." Clancy gave the chauffeur a great
many instructions, and explained at length that Mr.
Witherall was to be driven easy. "And when you get
back, let me know how he stood it, Carl."

Dow chuckled as the limousine rolled away.

"Too bad we didn't suggest breakfast. Drop a hat,
and Clancy'd have hitched on a camp kitchen. I don't
know what impressed Comrade Clancy more, your

broad A, or your pince-nez, or the Maharajah. Shakespeare, will you stretch your neck and gaze up at these snow banks? I hope someone's dug out your new house. If I know the beautiful little city of Dalton, the outlying districts are probably imbedded."

"Have you lived there long?" Leonidas inquired.

"You haven't, if you can ask me that," Dow said. "I've lived there all my life. Which reminds me, Mike's going to call on you—remember I said I had to wake Mike?"

Leonidas nodded.

"Well, it was your old pupil and crack miler, Mike Clayton. He didn't look you up on the train, because he was tearing off at Back Bay. That's how I happened to find your unconscious form. I was seeking you out to relay his regards, and I couldn't find you in your drawing room. I went back to see him after the lipstick hunt, and mentioned you— Shakespeare, I can't get rid of the feeling that you don't trust me."

"So you suggested to Mr. Clancy. Er—why?"

Dow shrugged.

"I don't know. I just feel it. The Dows are sensitive folk. Look, let's get to the core. Father was the Dow who ran the Dalton National Bank for twenty years. Mother is an ex-president of the Tuesday Club. I've got an uncle who's a bishop, and an aunt who gets blue ribbons at Cat Shows—doesn't that sound upright and respectable?"

"It's almost awe-inspiring," Leonidas said. "Particularly the aunt."

"You still—well, let's tackle it from the other side. Who do you know in Dalton?"

"Whom," Leonidas said. "Whom. I know all the Meredith faculty, now that the school's moved out there. I have good friends in the Kayes—"

"My own cousins."

"And Cassie Price—"

Dow whooped.

"My cousin Cassie! My favorite woman in all Dalton! Wait, wait—I've got it, now! Last week I met Cassie in Blaine's, buying a leather chair for someone named Bill whose new house she was overseeing! She just said Bill, not Bill Shakespeare, but it's you—you and your house, isn't it? There! Doesn't that make you feel better about me, to know I'm Cassie's third cousin, a couple of times removed?"

"It does," Leonidas said honestly. "But—"

"Did you know her husband?"

"No. Dow, I wish—"

"He and my dad played golf, and fished—dad used to say that Bagley Price was the only man he knew whose life was never dull. Do you know, Cassie never put his socks in the same place twice running, from the time she married him till he died? She claimed she wasn't going to let Bagley get in a mental rut, expecting the same thing, always."

"Cassie Price," Leonidas said, "is probably one of the more unexpected people. But suppose you tell me, Dow, exactly what—"

"How did you ever dare let *her* build your house?" Dow asked. "How did you *dare?*"

"You speak," Leonidas said, "as though Cassie constructed it with her bare hands, laying plank on plank and brick on brick. Which, of course, is not the case. She merely kept an eye on the architect, and saw that—"

"Isn't it crazy to think she's a grandmother? And young Jock's living with her this winter, too. His family's skiing in Switzerland, and they intended to take Jock. But he pretended to break his leg again."

"I know," Leonidas said. "He's broken bone after bone to escape skiing with his family. Dow, I should like to be told how it happened that you—"

"Jock adores Cassie, and she adores him. Did you ever hear—"

Without any visible pause, Dow told stories of Cassie Price till the black limousine rolled into Dalton.

"City limits," Dow said. "And wouldn't you know

it. My God, look at the snow! Will you look at it?"

"There seems," Leonidas said with resignation, "to be a lot of it."

He had given up trying to work a word in edgewise.

"Good old Dalton Street Cleaning Department. That's what we call it in our laughing way. The Street Cleaning Department. You won't be so calm and resigned about it, Bill, after you've paid a batch of Dalton taxes. My mother claims that the whole Department went on the last Byrd expedition, and no one ever noticed. The Street Cleaning Department is mother's pet topic, next to what does she pay taxes for, anyway, she'd like to know, if. You must meet mother. She'll throw a tea— Carl, can you get through Oak to Maple, and then swing up Walnut? Then Walnut to Lime."

Leonidas barely heard Dow's monologue about Dalton streets and the Street Cleaning Department, as it was laughingly called. His eyes were fixed on Birch Hill, looming beyond.

The car skidded to a stop.

"Stuck, Carl?" Dow demanded.

"Not yet, but we can't go no further. See? The road ain't plowed through to the next street. Only as far as the last house."

"Back up and turn around, and go back to Walnut," Dow called out as the rear wheels churned noisily. "Try Cherry to Elm. Elm ought to be clear. An alderman lives on Elm."

Elm, if anything, was worse.

"My God!" Dow said in disgust. "Well, go back another block, Carl. Try Pine to Poplar. We ought to be able to hit the hill road somewhere!"

Both Pine and Poplar proved to be virgin wastes of drifted snow.

"Well," Dow said, "try Sycamore to Eucalyptus. If we can't get through there, Shakespeare, you're sunk!"

Sycamore differed from Pine and Poplar in that an oil truck was half buried in the drifts, but Eucalyptus outdid them all. The snow plow was buried on Eucalyptus. A small boy informed them that it had been there for two days.

"That," Dow said to Leonidas, "is what we call the laissez-faire, or Dalton policy of city government. Let's see, now, what did we do with that orange snow plow? Oh, that old thing? We left that on Eucalyptus way back in the blizzard of eighty-eight! Shakespeare, that's that. You can't get to Birch Hill. If you must build houses, you ought to build on the lowlands, with the proletariat. Or wear snow shoes. Carl, turn back to—"

"Wait," Leonidas said. "The streets on the other side of the hill. What about them?"

"Them? Oh, they ain't plowed!" Carl said. "Not if these ain't."

Leonidas looked at Birch Hill.

"I think," he said, "we will try them. If you don't mind."

"Mister, there ain't no use!"

"Still," Leonidas said, "let us try them. Er—I wonder if you hear me, Carl?" The man's head jerked around. "Ah. You do. Carl, let's try the other side."

"Honest, mister, you can see from here, there ain't no sense trying!"

There was something about the expression on Carl's stolid face that reminded Leonidas suddenly of the porter who had become alarmed at the howdah, and of the people who had watched him come to on the green plush Pullman seat. It was the same thing, gentle, kindly tolerance for an elderly man who had been knocked out, and whose brain, through no particular fault of his own, was consequently on the addled side.

Belatedly, it occurred to Leonidas that Carl had been spoken to. Carl had been primed. There had been ample opportunity for it, back at the station. It had not been intended from the first that this expedition, whether it traveled in an ambulance or a limousine or a howdah, should ever come to rest at Number Forty Birch Hill Road.

"You tell him," Carl said to Dow.

"He's right, Shakespeare," Dow said. "I tell you, I know Dalton and the Street Cleaning Department. If this side's like this, the other side'll be worse. I know you're burning to see your house, but— Say, Shakespeare, I've got an idea! I tell you what we better do!"

"Indeed?"

Leonidas mentally sat back and prepared himself for the worst. He expected, at the very least, some suggestion of a private nursing home. Whatever had been decided, Leonidas felt, there was practically nothing that he could do about it.

"It's a whale of a thought!" Dow said with a rush of genial heartiness. "It's a wow!"

"Er—what?" Leonidas could almost feel the rush of air as spiked iron gates of a sanitorium swung closed behind him.

"Why, Cassie's! Let's go to Cassie's! She lives on Paddock Street— Bill, do you feel all right? You look as though you'd gulped a goldfish. You going to be sick, or anything?"

"Go on," Leonidas said in a strained voice.

"Paddock Street's just off the turnpike, and it'll be clear. It always is. Cassie wields some strange, mysterious power over the Street Cleaning Department. Mother says it's her homemade apricot cordial that she doles out as a reward, but I wouldn't know.

Don't you think that's a wow of an idea? We'll go to Cassie's, and take stock of the situation—and say, hasn't she got your keys, anyway?"

Leonidas studied the floor carpet, and then nodded.

"We should have thought of it in the first place," Dow said. "Paddock Street, Dalton Hills, Carl. Ninety-nine. Yes, Shakespeare, you can have her doctor look you over—you're looking a little white around the gills, you know, still. Then when you've rested up some, Cassie can either mesmerize the Street Cleaning Department into doing some plowing, or you can hire a sleigh. I've got a—a relation on Birch Hill who uses a sleigh all winter."

"Perhaps," Leonidas said slowly, "you're right. M'yes. You're quite right."

His tone convinced Dow, but anyone who knew Leonidas well would not have been deceived for a moment. The slow, measured twirling of the pince-nez was in itself a danger signal.

"But I feel," Leonidas went on, "that it would be a courteous gesture to warn Cassie. She may not even be up. Suppose you stop at the drugstore in Dalton Hills, and telephone her that we're coming? And while you're there, you can get me some Nivirin."

"Some what?"

"Nivirin," Leonidas said. "Headache powders. Much as I hate to confess it, my head has begun to throb most painfully. Nivirin—wait, I'll write it down for you." He drew out his wallet and a pencil from his pocket, and wrote busily on a calling card. "There. I've jotted down the prescription, in case the druggist doesn't have them, and I'm sure it won't take a moment to have it filled. Nivirin is an old compound, but I have every faith in it. It was devised by my old friend Dr. Livingston. I presume you've heard of him."

Leonidas caught himself just in time to keep from adding something about Mr. Stanley and Darkest Africa. That was the danger with the Maharajah touch. It ran away with you if you weren't careful.

But Dow didn't notice.

He took the card and gave Carl more directions, while Leonidas absently fingered his wallet and tried to look as wan and anguished as he could.

The instant that the Dalton Hills Pharmacy door closed behind Dow, Leonidas withdrew two ten-dollar bills from his wallet.

"Carl," he said in a weak voice, "you can't see the windows for the snow banks, but can you see a florist's sign across the street anywhere?"

There should be one. There ought to be one. There had to be one!

"Yeah. Over there," Carl said.

"Would you be willing to take this money and get

some roses? I want to take something to Mrs. Price, and I don't feel equal to going, myself."

"Sure." Carl's first quick look of suspicion at the sight of the bills instantly melted at Leonidas's plaintive request. Carl felt sorry for the poor old duffer. He hadn't stood the trip well, and that was a fact. "Sure. I'll get 'em. How many roses you want?"

"Get the best you can for the money," Leonidas said. "And, Carl, have them done up nicely, so they won't seem to be an afterthought. You know. Have them look like a present."

Carl nodded.

"Sure, mister, I know. With bows on the box. Okay."

Three minutes later, Leonidas was in a maroon-colored taxi, headed at a brisk clip toward Birch Hill.

They had been a very full three minutes, Leonidas thought with pleasure. He had accomplished a lot. He had covered a considerable amount of ground.

Screened by the towering snow banks, he had left the limousine, made his way with great rapidity through a network of snow-heaped alleys, and crossed three snow-banked streets before he hailed the maroon-colored taxicab.

In his pocket, furthermore, he had two keys.

One was the key to the limousine's ignition, which would curtail Carl and Dow for a while after they finished their respective errands.

The other was a key which had dropped unnoticed from Dow's coat pocket onto the car carpet while he was giving Carl instructions about streets. It was that key which had prompted Leonidas to take his present course.

For the key was tagged with a plainly visible tag, which said succinctly, "40 B.H.Rd. Witherall House."

Ten minutes later, Leonidas was staring at Number Forty Birch Hill Road from the sidewalk in front, where the maroon taxi had left him.

There was a house, and it was numbered Forty. He could see the numerals on the front door, and he could see the street sign of Birch Hill Road at the corner.

But Number Forty was no snug little cottage with peaked gables and green blinds.

Number Forty was an imposing modern functional house, flat-roofed, with sun decks and casement windows and inserts of glass brick.

Leonidas caught his breath.

Then he began to wonder what genius had fitted the house within the clumps of slender birches. Because it did fit. It fitted as if it had grown there on the hillside, always. The great elms were gone— Cassie had cabled that they were victims of the hurricane. But the tall evergreens growing in their places looked as if they, too, had been there always.

Leonidas smiled as he walked up the shoveled front

walk. He chuckled aloud as he read the builder's sign that sat rakishly on the doorstep.

> "Weaver & Briggs, Builders.
> C. W. Dow, Architect."

He began to understand, as he stared at the sign, the machinations of young Mr. Dow. Things began to clear up. The unpredictable Cassie Price had done the unexpected. She had junked his plans and hired Dow, and together they had built this house. Now they both had cold feet at the thought of the consequences.

It was entirely characteristic of Cassie to have planted Dow on his trail, to prepare him and break the shock.

Leonidas couldn't guess how Dow had managed to land on the train, but at any rate, Dow's role was plain. There was no longer any mystery surrounding his statement that no one would be meeting Leonidas at the station. Dow simply knew it.

For the rest, fate had played into Dow's hands. Or out of them, Leonidas amended, depending on your point of view. Fate had popped open the door of the empty drawing room and enabled Dow to render yeoman service to his unconscious form. Dow had nothing to do with the girl or the mousy woman or the person under the gray blankets, or with any of that confused, tantalizing episode. On the other hand, fate had also

aroused Leonidas's suspicions to such an extent that
Dow, realizing them, had no earthly opportunity of
bringing up in any graceful manner the matter of the
changed house.

There had been one moment, when they first met
in the corridor, but Dow had lost his nerve.

But neither Cassie nor Dow needed to go to such
elaborate lengths, Leonidas reflected as he tried the
key in the front door. Because he liked his new house.
He thought it was one of the loveliest things he had
ever seen in his life. He was delighted.

The key didn't fit the front door, so Leonidas followed the path around to the rear of the house. The
curved wall of a bay window fascinated him. He could
hardly wait to find out what it meant and what it was.

As he turned the key, he noticed the arbor vitae
hedge that formed a little enclosure to his left. Probably a terrace lay under the snow, he decided. A terrace
where he could sit and look over the winding James
River to the Carnavon Hills beyond.

The prospect pleased him. Leaving the key in the
lock, Leonidas started through the snow to investigate.
With what amounted to shame, he remembered that
the gabled cottage had a garage in that spot. He didn't
know why. He owned no car. But now he could sit on
his terrace, hidden from the street by the tree hedge,
and survey that beautiful view to his heart's content.

Suddenly, Leonidas stopped short in his tracks.

Someone was moving behind the hedge, creeping past the far corner. Someone had been watching him at the back door, and was now sneaking away at his unexpected advance.

Cassie, of course. Dow had probably telephoned her of his escape, and Cassie had set out at once for the hill.

"Cassie!" Leonidas started to wade through the snow. "Wait, Cassie! Don't run away! I like it! I think it's superb!"

He waded across the drifts of the terrace to cut off her retreat.

But she was too quick for him.

She was speeding down the front walk before Leonidas finished wriggling his way through the hedge. He wasn't very efficient in his wriggling, because he was dazed to a point where he couldn't co-ordinate very well.

The woman was not Cassie Price.

Leonidas almost couldn't believe his eyes. Because he had caught a fleeting but photographic glimpse of a face already etched forever on his memory.

It was the face of the mousy woman of the train.

CHAPTER III

A BRAWNY, mittened paw reached out and grabbed his shoulder as Leonidas started after her.

"Hold it, bud!"

Leonidas looked from the paw along a stretch of official blue coat sleeve to the massive Dalton policeman standing behind him.

"That woman!" Leonidas said urgently. "I've got to get that woman—"

"Tch, tch." The cop clucked his tongue in reproof. "Tch, tch!"

"Officer," Leonidas said, "if you won't let me chase that woman, won't you?"

"And if I don't fall for that one," the cop returned, "I suppose you got a baby for me to hold, huh?"

Leonidas put on his pince-nez.

"Exactly what do you mean, officer?"

"Listen, bud, don't get fresh with me! There wasn't no woman, and I ain't going to run off and chase her, and you ain't neither. I wasn't born yesterday!"

"There was a woman," Leonidas said. "A woman with whom I've had a peculiar and somewhat trying experience today."

The cop eyed him.

"I bet they just can't keep away from you, can they, bud?"

"Officer," Leonidas said, "that woman was watching me—"

"I been watching you too, see, bud? I seen you prowling around. I seen you try the front door. There's been enough of that around here. So you come along with me."

"My name," Leonidas said, "is Witherall. This happens to be my house."

The cop found that statement hilariously funny, and he said so.

"And, bud," he lowered his voice, "don't never breathe it to a soul, but my name's Windsor. I own Buckingham Palace, myself."

Leonidas fumbled in the inner pocket of his coat.

"Here," he said, "is my wallet, and here is my passport. If those don't convince you of my identity, perhaps you'd be good enough to call your chief. Tell Colonel Carpenter that you're holding a personal friend of his."

The cop looked at the passport, and winced.

"Ooop!" he said. "Sorry. Keeping a watch on this

place was the colonel's idea. We was supposed to pay special attention to this house. I didn't know you was home yet. You see, you're still on the vacant-house list. I'll take you off when I go back to report."

"Thank you," Leonidas said. "Perhaps you'll report my return to the colonel, personally, will you? Tell him I appreciate your watchfulness and—er—zeal. And if Cuff Murray's still on the force, tell Cuff I'm home."

"Cuff's on sick leave—you know Cuff?"

"Cuff," Leonidas said, "is also a personal friend."

The cop choked back whatever comment he had on the tip of his tongue.

"Friend, huh? That so. He certainly is a big boy, Cuff is. Built like a stadium. He's sure a big fellow."

"Physically speaking, Cuff is a remarkable specimen," Leonidas said. "Mentally—er, tell me. How did he get on the force? It happened while I was away, and I've been very curious to know. He's a protégé of Mrs. Price's, but I didn't want to ask her. I didn't want her to know that I doubted his ability to read."

"He can, all right. He passed his exams high. Then of course he's a swell shot—he stopped a bank robber last month. And he's athaletic. And honest, I never seen a guy pick up so many stolen cars!"

Leonidas smiled. That was not unusual, in view of

Cuff's former occupation. Cuff had stolen cars for a living.

"I know Mrs. Price was rooting for him, but that wouldn't cut any ice with the colonel," the cop went on. "Cuff got his rating. Me, I never thought he could pass. I'll have Sweeny tell him you're home."

Leonidas extracted a bill from his wallet.

"Thank you. And there was a woman, you know. There really was. Lurking behind the hedge, and peeking at me as I unlocked the door."

"Peeking around, huh? Well, I wouldn't give it a second thought, Mr. Witherall. There's been an awful lot of people come to look at this house of yours. It's different from any other house in Dalton, see, and that made 'em curious. A lot of women come to look at it, particularly with Mrs. Price around so much. I spoke to the colonel about it, but he just said if I could manage his sister Cassie, I was a better man than him. You know how Mrs. Price is. She knows everybody."

Leonidas nodded.

He wanted to say that he was aware of Cassie Price's vast circle of acquaintances, but that this woman was different.

This woman, he wanted to say, was the woman who cracked me over the head on the train this morning.

This was the woman who hid a gun and a pair of handcuffs in the water cooler. The woman who rushed off the train at Back Bay with a beautiful girl. The woman who left me for dead on the floor of Drawing Room B, and apparently caused a body under those gray blankets to dissolve into thin air.

But he couldn't say it. However clear all those facts were in his own mind, they were nothing to throw casually at a cop, even to one of Colonel Carpenter's cops.

"In and out, in and out, all the time," the cop said. "Those women! Look, you can't see no special tracks in the snow. She just walked around where the men walked that knocked the snow off your trees. The fellows that shoveled. They're the Italians that do Mrs. Price. The woman was just gawping around, Mr. Witherall. Something to gawp at, too. That's a fine house you got there. I wish I owned that heater of yours. Let me know if there's ever anything I can do. Peters in Car Fifteen. We hang out around the hill. So long."

"Wait," Leonidas said. "Tell me about the snow-removal system. For the streets, I mean. I notice that Main Avenue was clear, but what about all those streets on the other side of the hill, like Elm and Lime and Cherry?"

"Them? Oh, they're unfinished streets. Did you try

to come up that way? You can later on, over the rough ends, but they only plow as far as the last house. Couple of 'em ain't accepted streets, so they ain't plowed till last. Just use Main. The rest of the hill here's always fixed up. Let me know if it ain't. Good-by, now."

All thoughts of the mousy woman erased themselves from Leonidas's mind as he entered his house.

The kitchen was a gay, shining room, with red and gray linoleum floor and walls. His glance jumped from the highly burnished copper pots and pans on a wall rack to closets and cupboards, and the potted plant on the window sill.

There seemed to be a lot of red things running in an unbroken line around the walls. One, with slashes of chromium, was a stove. A lot of the others were red linoleum tops to cupboards and drawers, which formed a sort of working space, Leonidas decided. One red thing turned into a sort of sink, when the metal cover was raised, an amazing sink with an electric dishwasher and a garbage chopper tucked away in it.

Leonidas set both going, and listened with pleasure to the motors humming.

But of all the red things, the prize was the red refrigerator. He opened the door, and the interior instantly lighted up, a phenomenon which almost caused Leonidas to crow. Probably a floodlighted red refrigerator was a hackneyed, commonplace fixture to the

average housewife, but to Leonidas it was both satisfactory and thrilling. He opened and closed the door
half a dozen times for the sheer joy of watching the
light go on.

Then he realized that the refrigerator, like the cup-
board shelves, was stocked with food. Eggs, butter, a
magnificent cooked Virginia ham.

"What," Leonidas said, "am I waiting for?"

He unearthed coffee and a coffeepot, mastered the
intricacies of the electric stove, and proceeded to cook
himself some breakfast.

He wanted to see the rest of the house. He yearned
to see it. But if the rest were as satisfactory as this
room, he would never be able to pause for food.

It disappointed him to find the chef's cap and apron
after he had finished cooking, but he put the outfit
on anyway, and wondered whether Dow or Cassie or
Jock was responsible for the legend, "Bill's Chop
House," stitched on the front. There was a red telephone in the corner, and he started to phone Cassie
and invite everybody to breakfast. But a telephone
conversation with Cassie, as he knew from experience,
was nothing to be entered into lightly. It was something you undertook when you had a clear, free day
ahead. And he wanted to see the rest of the house. And
besides, they were probably on their way.

He returned things to the refrigerator lingeringly,

one at a time, put his dishes in the washer, and fed coffee grounds and eggshells to the garbage chopper.

Just as he opened the red refrigerator door for one last time before setting out to see the rest of the house, a musical chime began to sound in a gentle, restrained fashion.

Leonidas finally tracked it down. It was the bell at the rear entrance.

He wondered, as he opened the door, what the front door would produce. An aria, probably.

A man with a piece of paper in his hand stood on the doorstep.

He looked at Leonidas's cap and apron, and then thrust out the paper.

"We got an icebox, mister."

"That's nice," Leonidas said.

"For you."

"Thank you, I have one. It's red, and it lights up."

"Yeah, but it ain't right—"

"My dear fellow," Leonidas said, "it is. Definitely. It's just the thing."

"Listen, I tell you we got an icebox!"

"I don't doubt it. I'm sure you have, if you say so."

"Listen, yours ain't right, see? Yours is all wrong. Yours don't work."

"My good man," Leonidas said, "it works beautifully. I know. I've worked it. It's a fine red refrigerator, and it satisfies me completely. As far as I am concerned, the refrigerator problem has been solved, and I am not in the market for more refrigerators. Good morning."

"Don't you want a bigger one?"

"No."

"But this one's a better one than you got!"

"Impossible. Good morning!"

"Listen, I'm supposed to take your icebox out—"

"What?" Leonidas put on his pince-nez. "You're supposed to what?"

"Take your icebox out, see?" the man waved the paper. "I'm supposed to take your icebox out, and—"

"The person," Leonidas said firmly, "who removes my red refrigerator will do so over my dead body. Is that quite clear?"

He shut the door.

He remembered that Cassie had often complained bitterly of the number of people who came to her house and tried to sell her things, but he hadn't suspected that anything as large as refrigerators would be peddled from door to door. The fellow was obviously a half-wit.

He paused a moment in the kitchen, and then took the door at his right. The front of the house would probably prove most interesting, so he would save that till last.

He found himself in the most fantastic room he had ever seen in his life. It wasn't large, but it contained a gas furnace, a washing machine, a drier, a hot-water heater, and several large boxlike objects whose purpose he didn't even dare guess at. One of them, he suspected, conditioned air. If it didn't, it was a rocket ship.

A door in the corner led down a short flight of steps to a small hallway, and Leonidas realized for the first time that the slope of the hill had been utilized to provide for a lower level. He hadn't noticed it, with the drifts outside.

On the right was a low-ceilinged bedroom with a bath beyond. A servant's room, Leonidas decided, and very ingenious of Mr. Dow. Its occupant could come and go without disturbing anyone, and the tiny radio could run forever without any complaints from him.

He returned to the hallway and hurried along to the door on the left.

It was sealed with a wide strip of rather grimy adhesive tape, under which a note had been stuck.

Leonidas smiled as he put on his pince-nez and read the scrawl.

"Dear Bill,
    Please don't go in here till I come. Please. Don't let Gran invaiggle you, either. This is in case anything goes wrong with our plans and I'm not here

when you are. Please wait. This is my surprise as much
as theirs. I thought of it.

Jock."

Leonidas chuckled. Jock knew, better than anyone, how his grandmother could inveigle. And Jock, in
turn, was probably the only person who exerted any
real influence over his impetuous grandmother. Cassie
was putty in Jock's hands.

Probably the room would be a workshop, he thought
as he went back upstairs. Jock and his uncle, Colonel
Carpenter, built model ships, and very likely the workshop had been their idea. Leonidas could imagine that
Cassie, who hated what she called their litter, had
enthusiastically approved the plan. Whatever the
motives, it was nice to have a workroom in one's house.

He hurried through the boiler room and the kitchen
into a small dining room, with a bay window of glass
brick at one end. It would never suit a person like
Cassie, who was unhappy without at least eight to
dinner, but it was large enough for Leonidas, and
his old mahogany table fitted beautifully against the
wall. He liked the inlaid linoleum floor, and the built-in
china shelves.

The dining room led to a hall, from which a circular
staircase rose. Leonidas paused, and then crossed the
hall into a living room that ran the width of the house.

He stood in the doorway and held his breath.

A long glass picture window looked out over the terrace. There was a fireplace to his left, with a low, curving sort of sofa in front of it. There was a large green leather chair that contrasted strikingly with the mulberry-colored broadloom carpet. There was his favorite old desk in the corner.

Leonidas sat down in the leather chair and continued to drink in details. The phonograph radio. The Sargent portrait of his grandfather over the fireplace. His grandfather had been a particularly unpleasant man who never said a kindly word or did a kindly thing, but he looked splendid hung on the wall.

An envelope fell off the leather chair arm. Leonidas picked it up and drew out a card.

"Colonel Rutherford Carpenter, United States Marine Corps, Retired," had been scratched out. On the back was a message.

"Cassie says you need this. Please accept it as a token of my esteem at having kept my sister out of jail for the record space of ten months."

No one, Leonidas thought with a rush of emotion, had any nicer friends.

Only one thing bothered him. Cassie had apparently wangled all his worldly possessions from the storage warehouse, but so far he had seen no books. Where were his books?

He crossed the hall and opened the door directly opposite.

"Ah!" he said. "Ah!"

Shelves of books rose from the floor to the ceiling, two stories up. That was all there was in the room, just shelves and shelves of books. Except for a flat-topped natural wood desk, built into a little enclosure at one corner.

There was a sign beside the inkwell.

"From Dow, who designed it."

Leonidas glowed.

If this sort of thing kept up much longer, he was going to dissolve into tears.

He kept wondering how one got to the top shelves, when he suddenly became aware of the ladder. Then, with a cry of pleasure, he discovered the tracks that ran around the linoleum floor, close to the shelves.

It was like a shoe-store ladder. It ran around.

Then Leonidas opened his mouth and hooted.

It was electric!

Climbing the ladder, he pressed the starter button.

Around and around the room he rolled until at last he took a firm grip on himself and turned off the motor.

"Wholeheartedly," Leonidas said, "I approve of this house!"

He was about to telephone Cassie Price and assure

her on that point when the back-door chimes sounded again.

It was the man who had been there before.

"Listen, mister," he said before Leonidas had a chance to speak, "you don't understand. You got the wrong icebox, see? And I got sent to take it back and give you the right one. You got a cheap one. You paid for a better one. More high-priced, see?"

"I don't want it."

"But you ain't got the right one. You got a cheap model, see?"

"My good man," Leonidas said, "let's have no more loose talk about the refrigerator situation. If a more expensive one was ordered and paid for, cause me to be sent a check for the difference. I am perfectly satisfied. Is that clear?"

"You mean, you don't want it?"

"If ever a nail," Leonidas said, "was squarely hit, you have hit it. I am satisfied. I don't wish another refrigerator. Furthermore," he added, "it is not my desire to see more of you. Be gone."

"Huh?"

"Scram," Leonidas said.

He had hardly time to open and close the red refrigerator half a dozen times when bells began to ring.

Leonidas never batted an eye. After the refrigerator

and the ladder, it seemed only natural that his front-door bell should merrily inform him that the Campbells were coming, tra la, tra la.

It was Cassie and Dow, of course.

Leonidas put on his pince-nez, adjusted his chef's cap to a rakish angle, and swung the door open wide.

A man stood there, urgently holding out a brush.

Leonidas took it.

"Are you the lady of the house, sir?"

"Er—yes. Yes, I suppose I am."

The man laughed. Somehow, he was inside the hall.

Half an hour later, Leonidas closed the door, and surveyed, with something akin to bewilderment, the mound of brushes on the floor. If the refrigerator man had been like that brush man, he thought, his kitchen would resemble a glacier.

He picked up the brushes and thrust them into a hitherto undiscovered hall closet.

The back-door chimes rang.

This time, Leonidas looked out the window before opening the door.

It was that man again!

He opened the door a crack.

"Do you," he said, "know Mr. Peters?"

"Huh?"

"Mr. Peters, of the Prowl Car Fifteen Peterses? Because if you stay there a few minutes longer, you will have an excellent opportunity of meeting Mr. Peters. I have summoned him."

He strode back into the kitchen and picked up the red phone.

Simultaneously, the Campbells started coming from the front door.

Perhaps this was the sort of thing Cassie referred to when she said that what with people and door bells, she never had a minute to herself.

There was a coupé parked out front. This had to be Cassie and Dow!

But it was a large, well-girthed woman, staggering under the weight of a laden market basket whose handle flaunted a vivid purple bow.

Behind her, similarly burdened, was a woman Leonidas knew, and one of the few people in the world whom he actively disliked. He endured Estelle Otis only because she happened to be the wife of his friend and former colleague, Charles Otis, who still taught at Meredith's. Estelle was the only person Leonidas had ever met who never betrayed the slightest glimmer of a sense of humor.

Both women brushed by him and deposited their baskets on the floor.

"Ah, Leonidas," Estelle said. "This is Judge Round. Judge Harriet Pomeroy Round. You have heard of her. Hattie, she got the green drapes, after all!"

"Not really!"

"I wonder about the spreads. *I* said pink. I told her pink. Nothing but pink would do."

Without further ado, Estelle and Judge Round proceeded up the circular staircase.

Leonidas watched them with mounting irritation. Then he shrugged and sat down on the bottom step. There wasn't anything he could do about them. You couldn't actively boot from your house a lady judge, or the wife of one of your oldest friends. But at least he wouldn't give them the satisfaction of a personally conducted tour.

They finally came down, rather heatedly discussing whether a nice yellow wouldn't have been better than that rose, and pink or maybe even corn color better than the green. They thought the blue was definitely out of the question.

"What do you think?" Judge Round asked him brightly. "Tell us your opinion!"

But neither of them waited for it. Estelle said with relish that the blue would fade.

Judge Round, with equal relish, agreed.

Both of them thought that dear Cassie had probably done her best, but it was a pity about that pink.

"Pink wouldn't have faded," Estelle said. "Well, Leonidas, come see us. I'm sure your electric bills will be enormous, but I suppose you know what you're doing. It's a great mercy that your Uncle Orrin's estate was so large. You always did have spendthrift ways. All those books!"

"Do give my regards to Charles," Leonidas said. "Er —the baskets. You're forgetting them."

"Oh, it's the Welcome Committee. Dear me, I've forgotten the speech. It's been so long since I've done this. Do you remember the speech, Hattie?"

Judge Round smiled.

"Welcome to Dalton, Mr. Witherall," she said in the measured, fully rounded tones of an experienced clubwoman. "Welcome to Dalton, the Garden City, the City of Spotless Homes and Flowering Gardens. We hope your life here will be full and happy, that your children will spend happy, carefree hours in our lovely parks and modern playgrounds. Your children—"

"You'd best skip that part about children," Estelle interrupted. "We're in a hurry, and besides, he hasn't any."

Judge Round said that was stupid of her, wasn't it?

"Anyway, Mr. Witherall, we know you will find in our fair city every opportunity to carry on in peace and quiet your scholarly research."

"What research?" Leonidas inquired. No one in his right mind could ever refer to the Lieutenant Haseltine series as scholarly research.

"With all those books," Judge Round said, "we

know you're up to *something!* And Dalton's just the
proper, quiet, restful place. Isn't it, Estelle?"

"It is, up here. I told Charles I couldn't stand living so far away from things. Two miles from a loaf
of bread!"

"But the solitude! Think of the lovely solitude!"
Judge Round said. "Just the place for inspiration and
all that sort of thing. We know, Mr. Witherall, that
you will find much happiness in your little haven. So,"
she consulted her watch, "so it gives me great pleasure
to welcome you, on behalf of Dalton and our civic
organizations, including the Tuesday Club and the
Republican Club, and the—"

"The rest don't matter," Estelle said. "We do all
the work, anyway. I think it's a shame the others get
their names in. Well, Leonidas, there are tags on
everything," she pointed to the beribboned hampers,
"telling where they came from and who donated them,
and you're supposed to trade there. Give him the cards,
Hattie. We really didn't expect you'd be home, Leonidas. We just rang to hear the tune. We intended to
put the things inside the hall, and go."

"Come, Estelle," the judge said hurriedly. "Come.
Good-by, Mr. Witherall. We hope you will be very
happy in your restful haven."

Leonidas cocked an eyebrow as he watched the
coupé being laboriously backed and turned.

So they were just going to put the things inside the hall, were they? That implied the possession of a key. He would speak sharply to Cassie, and have her recall any keys that she might have doled out in her enthusiasm. Cassie should have known better than to let Estelle Otis poke her nose inside his house.

He turned and looked at the hampers.

The contents ran the gamut from bottles of silver polish and astringent lotion to a tasteful bouquet of vegetables, from packets of flower seeds to boxes of steel wool, and an assortment of literature from the Dalton Chamber of Commerce.

The bunch of cards tied with purple ribbon, which the judge had thrust in his hand, was even more bizarre. By presenting one card or another, he was entitled to a free permanent wave at Madame Sade's, ten gallons of free gasoline, a free window cleaning, a free lawn mowing, a free floor polishing, a free dental examination with the first cavity filled free, a free palm reading at the Dalton Gipsy Tea Shoppe, and a free evening of bowling at Dinty's Tavern and Snack Bar Bowling Alleys.

Leonidas dumped both the hampers and the cards into the hall closet, along with the mound of brushes.

Then he made two neat signs that said, "I LIKE IT," and put one in a front window, and one in the kitchen window. That was to reassure Cassie and Dow.

Then he hurried up the circular stairs.

A luxuriously stocked linen closet caught his eye. He felt the texture of a blue percale sheet, and wondered if perhaps Cassie hadn't gone a little too far with the monograms. Everything in sight, including the face cloths and the box of colored soap, bore his initials.

He investigated two small guest rooms separated by a bath, and the large room and bath which he decided must be his own. The bathrooms, with their colored fixtures and gleaming chromium taps, definitely awed him until he noticed two small sailboats in the green tub off his bedroom. If Jock could sail boats in that Lucullan thing, Leonidas thought, he certainly should feel unruffled about taking a bath in it.

His old spool bed in the bedroom looked strange to him, and he tried to figure out why. For one thing, it had been refinished. But it looked higher up, somehow, and less bumpy.

He sat on it, tentatively.

A new mattress. That was it.

He swung his legs upon the spread, stretched out, and looked through the casement windows over the sun deck to the Carnavon Hills.

It was very restful and very comfortable.

Maybe his new house was going to turn out to be a restful haven, after all.

The afternoon sun was streaming through the windows when he was awakened, several hours later, by a series of war whoops.

Cassie and Dow had finally arrived.

"Bill!" Cassie's startlingly snow-white hair brushed his face as she kissed him enthusiastically. "Bill, you really *do* like it? Really! Oh, you found the cap and apron! Dow, I told you he'd be here!"

"Bed," Dow perched on the railing of it, "was the only place you never did think of, Cassie. You never said a word about bed!"

"I told you he'd come here to the house! Oh, Bill, we're so glad you like it. We've been simply wretched for ten days, haven't we, Dow? We never set out to do this, Bill. It grew on us. And we never realized how far it had grown till we got the cable saying you were coming home— Did you have a good trip?"

Leonidas shrugged.

"So-so. We nearly got bombed in the Mediterranean, and we nearly got bombed in the Baltic, and there was talk of our being annihilated in Singapore, but nothing came of it. Things have been much more exciting since I left New York— Cassie, where have you been, you two? I thought you'd come here at once."

"We've been hunting you in hospitals," Dow said. "We'll probably all get measles. We wandered into a contagious ward, once."

Leonidas wanted to know why.

"Oh, just after you skipped from the limousine—and a nice skip it was, too. Very neat. Anyway, just afterwards, there was an accident up at the four corners in Dalton Hills. A Birch Hill-Carnavon bus turned over, and they told me that someone passing by had taken a man with a beard off to a hospital. Do you really like it? Honestly? You're not mad? What do you think of the place, really?"

Leonidas told them, at some length.

"I feel reborn," Dow said when he concluded. "I've lost ten pounds in the last month, and mother says I've worn a groove in the rugs from pacing around of nights, brooding over what we'd done. We didn't mean to, Bill. It all started so—so innocently! I just happened to drop into Cassie's."

"I know," Leonidas said. "I know."

"You can't know!" Cassie said. "It was the day after I got your cable saying to get the house plans from your lawyer, and tell the architect to start building, and all. And Dow dropped in, and he called the architect's office, and he'd died. So I asked Dow if he couldn't oversee things, and he said yes. And we liked your cottage, Bill. We really did. Did you notice how we kept the floor plan? Of course, we moved the living room, and swung out the ell for the boiler room, and added the terrace, and changed the levels, and the kitchen and dining room are different—"

"Otherwise," Leonidas said, "it's the same?"

"Well, we kept the linen closet at the head of the stairs," Cassie said defensively. "That's just where it was in your cottage. Really, we didn't *not* like your cottage, Bill. But we got to looking at the hillside, and thinking, and then we thought of little changes here, and little changes there."

Dow and Leonidas found themselves grinning at each other.

"I understand, Cassie," Leonidas said. "And as far as I'm concerned, you need never mention that—er— that corny cottage again."

"Isn't that amazing!" Cassie said. "We all thought it was pretty corny, too. But of course, we'd never have said so in a million years. Anyway, the thing grew on us, and then we got scared, and I sent Dow over to New York to prepare you, and he went early because he had other business, and it was simply God's grace that he spotted you while he was walking down to the train with Mike Clayton last night. Of course, he should have let me know then—"

"I had fifteen minutes," Dow said, "to check out of the hotel and catch that train, Cassie, as I've told you and *told* you! I think it's to my credit that I caught it."

"You could have sent a telegram," Cassie returned.

"And then there wouldn't have been all that nonsense at the station. There wouldn't have been any nonsense at all, if you'd only kept your wits about you when he started talking about his dream house! But you lost your nerve and ran away!"

"Some of the nonsense was inevitable," Leonidas said. "You see, Dow, after you ran away, a woman—"

"He bungled things, Bill," Cassie said. "I should have gone to New York, myself. Look, have you thought of anything we forgot?"

"Just one. A sign to ward off peddlers. You can't imagine how many peddlers and callers I've had. There was a brush man who sold me a carload lot of strange assorted brushes. And—"

"Didn't you find the talker?" Dow interrupted. "A round thing at the door, like a tea-strainer. Well, you press a button, and chat with the person on the doorstep before you let 'em in. It's great fun. Cassie sassed the bishop and made a date with the vegetable man. Come on down, and we'll demonstrate."

"I wish," Leonidas said as they trooped downstairs, "that you'd demonstrate the brushes. They all seemed so logical when that man showed them to me, but there's one squiggly worm of a thing with a curved handle that's been worrying me ever since the fellow left. I can't imagine what you'd do with such a diabolical object."

"Is it like this?" Cassie made motions. "With a sort of dent right along in here? Oh, I've got one of those. They're marvelous. That's what we fish Jock's kites from phone wires with. And there's another like it, only not so squiggly. It's called a Senior Bath Aid, but we use it to spread food over the pool for the goldfish. Let me see the rest, Bill. Where are they?"

Leonidas pointed to the closet, and Cassie opened the door.

"Oh!" she said. "Oh, my! Oh, dear!"

"I know I got too many, but he was such an efficient salesman, I never realized what an accumulation—"

"These hampers!" Cassie said in agonized tones. "Bill, has Estelle Otis been here already? She has! Oh dear me!"

"She came with some lady judge," Leonidas said. "And, while I think to ask, is it possible that Estelle has a key to this house?"

Dow and Cassie exchanged looks.

"Now we come to the hard part," Dow said. "Cassie, this is your department. Go on. Tell him."

"Don't tell me," Leonidas said, "that Estelle holds a mortgage, or something like that!"

"No, but you see, the house cost—"

"Considerably more than was planned. I know," Leonidas said. "I've already gathered that. About three times the original figure, wasn't it?"

Cassie's nod shattered his hope that he had over-estimated the deficit.

"Just about. But it doesn't cost you a cent more. You get four dollars and sixty-three cents back. Give him the check, Dow. There! That's how Estelle happened to have a key. See?"

Leonidas shook his head.

"Well, it was my idea. We got the best of everything for practically nothing," Cassie said happily. "We got the gas things and the electric things at cost for letting the gas and electric people demonstrate them, and hold cooking classes, and lectures, and all."

"Er—here?" Leonidas asked.

"Yes. And because Rutherford got the nurseries a big city tree order, then we got all your trees and shrubs free. And then we got the street and sewer assessments cut for letting the mayor make a speech and say this was Dalton the Garden City's answer to the challenge of modern progress and housing. We had Dalton Day."

"Er—here?"

"Yes. Rutherford had to call out his Emergency Strike and Riot Squad, there were so many people. Then Blaine's did the linoleum and the decorating and the furniture for almost nothing, and then they used it as a demonstration model. But they were awfully careful, Bill. Everything was roped off, and people weren't let touch a thing. And the linens and the kitchen furnishings and dishes are from the Tuesday Club, in return for their study of modern housing."

"You mean that the Tuesday Club actually came here and studied this house?"

"They just camped here," Cassie said. "They gave you the doorbell chimes, too, and Mrs. Pettingill's husband got the radios wholesale. And Estelle correlated all the findings and wrote them up in a paper. She called it The House Moderne. That's why she had a key. But you've got four dollars and sixty-three cents left, Bill. Isn't that fine?"

Leonidas laughed until the tears rolled down his cheeks.

"I think it's the funniest thing I ever heard! So that's why the cop knew about the furnace, and why those two women— Oh, my! Is there anyone in Dalton who didn't have a hand in the building of my house?"

"I don't think so," Dow said. "All of Dalton and Carnavon and the surrounding towns have seen it at least twice. We never planned it as a community venture. It somehow just got to be one. And you really don't mind?"

"After that superb refrigerator and the library ladder," Leonidas said, "I could forgive almost anything. Dow, before we get sidetracked on the door-talker gadget, tell me something. On the train—"

"Wait," Dow said. "While he's in such a receptive mood, Cassie, hadn't we better tell him about the other trouble?"

Cassie nodded. "Let's get it over with. It's about a woman, Bill."

"A mousy woman?" Leonidas asked eagerly.

"Merciful heavens, no! She's a ramping termagant. Whatever made you think she was a mousy woman?"

"Well," Leonidas said, "on the train this morning there was a beautiful girl, and also a—"

"That girl!" Cassie said. "I'm so sick of hearing about her. Dow's talked of nothing else. Was she really beautiful?"

"She really was. And with her—"

"It took all the sterling in my character not to ditch you on the train, Bill, and chase after her," Dow said. "That girl is going to be my life work. After I get you and your house settled, I'm going to find that girl and marry her."

"I wish Estelle Otis could hear you say that!" Cassie said darkly. "She'd make hash of you. Bill, Dow is engaged to Elsa Otis. Isn't that awful?"

"Hideous," Leonidas said promptly. He knew Elsa. Elsa was a buck-toothed replica of her mother. "How did it ever happen?"

"I can't think," Cassie said. "Dow doesn't seem to know, either. He's miserable about it, and there's nothing he can do. Estelle won't ever let one of the Dows slip out of her family. She's already approached the bishop about the wedding."

"I should be inclined to blackmail the bishop, myself," Leonidas said. "Is Elsa the ramping termagant you mentioned, Cassie?"

"That dumpy thing? Oh, no! The trouble is with your next-door neighbor. That is, she's not very next-door, but she's the nearest neighbor you have. She says this house is hideous, and loathsome beyond belief, and you spoil her view, and she's going to drive you out."

"Those," Leonidas said, "are the ravings of a jealous woman. It's nothing but jaundiced envy. No sane woman could say such things. She can't mean it."

"Well," Dow said, "I didn't think she did at first. But then she disinherited me. You see, she's an aunt of mine. That is, she's an aunt of my mother's. I was named for her favorite brother. Chauncey Winthrop. That's why I prefer to be called just Dow. She's pretty sore, and she's been doing a lot of ominous muttering. It all boils down to the fact that she has decided to drive you out."

"Nonsense," Leonidas said. "How can she?"

"Legally, she can't. The land title is clear all the way back to Chief Big Toe, and the house complies with the building codes and housing regulations. I've had half of City Hall up here trying to find a single thing that she could rightfully carp about, and there's not one. On the other hand, Bill, I've got a nasty feeling that Aunt Medora will find some nasty way of annoying you. She's a master harrier. She's renowned for her harrying."

"Her name is Medora?"

"Uh-huh. Mehitable Dora, but she turned it into Medora. She's mother's aunt, but she's not much older than mother. She was grandmother's youngest—"

"What does she look like?" Leonidas twirled his pince-nez casually.

"She's an old harridan!" Cassie said. "Her teeth click, and she wears a red wig. She's a horrible woman! She dresses like a jitterbug. She's rich as Croesus, and she's capable of anything. When she got mad at the Country Club last year, she bought up all that expensive land on the west boundary, and set men to blasting there, all day long. People went crazy trying to play golf, and they had to stop polo entirely. And finally some of the men formed a syndicate, and bought the land back at a fabulous price. That's just an example of what the old harridan can do!"

"Has the colonel been told of these mutterings?" Leonidas asked.

"Certainly," Dow said. "Officially, he can't take

steps because we have no specific complaint, but he's had his men keep watch, and Car Fifteen usually parks right around the corner. And we insured the house against all forms of damage and disaster and sabotage. I talked with Judge Round— Did you say she came here with La Otis?"

"She did," Leonidas told him. "She welcomed me to Dalton. She hoped my children would have fun in the municipal sand boxes. She called this place my restful haven, and wanted to know when I was starting the Great American Novel— Where did she pick up the idea that I was a literary gent?"

Cassie sighed. "I'm afraid that's my fault. People kept asking me why you had so many books, and they seemed to want a reason, so I just said you wrote. And they assumed I meant books—but Hattie Round's no fool, Bill. She's pretty clubby, but that's how she got along. And she's too clever to stop being clubby."

"You see, Bill," Dow said, "Our Own Dear Harriet Pomeroy Round is still on the up, and the gals are her biggest asset, so she coos a lot. But she's no dope. She gets along with the gals, and with Aunt Medora, which is almost unique. I had mother help Hattie in some Tuesday Club intrigue, and Hattie promised she'd speak a few warning words to Aunt Medora. Counter-propaganda. Like if the old girl got fresh, we'd go at her with a pickax, and knock her teeth out. Of course, it was better put, but that was the idea. But now, Bill, I wonder—"

"What?"

"Well, after seeing you mesmerize those red-faced gents on the train, I wonder—you'd ought to have heard him, Cassie, talking in a broad A about his pal the Maharajah. They were like to swoon."

"Did he?" Cassie looked suspiciously at Leonidas. "He talked about Maharajahs?"

"It slew 'em," Dow went on. "Look, suppose Bill took Hattie and went to call on Aunt Medora, and twinkled his blue eyes, and chatted about Maharajahs —why, he'd charm the pants off her, Cassie!"

"For my part," Leonidas said, "the policy of appeasement has never appealed to me. If your Aunt Medora blasts rocks at me, I shall not wave umbrellas at her reprovingly. Tell me, do you think it was wise under the circumstances to let keys to the house get into circulation?"

"It was then," Cassie said. "She never said a word at first. Only after the house was built. Bill, I forgot to ask, but you didn't look at Jock's surprise, did you? Oh, I'm so glad! He spent last night with Tim Adams, so he mercifully wasn't home when Dow phoned me from the station early this morning, or I'd never have got him to school. I haven't called him, either, because he'd be sure to skip, and I'm certain he'll come here on his way home— What time is it? Quarter to three? He'll be here soon."

"He likes Meredith's?"

"Loves it. Oh, dear, that's going to mean more explaining when his family get home. He was supposed to be sent to that progressive school in Carnavon, but he got expelled the first day— Did I write you about that? Didn't I? It was awfully hard on me. I didn't think it would take him an hour, but it took nearly three. And there was I parked around the corner waiting for him, a broiling hot day, and I got two tickets for parking. Bill, what made you so suspicious of Dow on the train? You must have been terribly suspicious, if you prattled about your old friend the Maharajah! What else happened?"

At long last, Leonidas thought, he was going to be able to tell his story about the mousy woman.

"Come into the living room," he said. "I'd begun to despair—"

A key turned the front-door latch, and Jock bounded in.

"Bill!" He hugged Leonidas. "Bill, I just made the Lower School Swimming Team! Did you look?"

"At your surprise? Certainly not!"

"I felt you'd be home early." Jock's overshoes and coat hit the corner simultaneously. "I told Gran you'd take the fast boat—come on! Come see it!"

Leonidas allowed himself to be rushed through the kitchen and boiler room, down the stairs to the lower hall.

Jock stopped short at the sealed door, and his face grew sober.

"Oh, Bill! You looked!"

"But I didn't, Jock! I read your note, and went back upstairs. Truly."

"The tape's been moved," Jock said. "See? Did you go in, Gran?"

"No, darling. If anyone's moved it, Uncle Root did last night. He brought over snow shovels and tools, don't you remember? Take off the tape, and show Bill. He hasn't seen a thing."

Reassured, Jock pulled off the strip of adhesive.

"Ready, Bill? Stand right here, so you can see when I swing the door open— Are you excited?"

"I'm panting," Leonidas said truthfully.

"One, two—ready? Three!"

The open door revealed a neat garage, in which a Bantam beach wagon proudly stood.

"And your name on the door!" Jock said. "It's from Gran and me. Do you like it? Don't you think it's the keenest thing?"

Leonidas didn't answer.

Over the wheel of the beach wagon was slumped the body of a woman.

"Don't you like it?" Cassie crowded into the doorway beside him. "You needed a car, living away up—away—oh, Bill!"

"What's the matter?" Dow peered over Leonidas's shoulder. "I think it's the snappiest model I—wow!"

The three of them stood in the doorway, surveying with horror the woman's disarranged red wig.

And the pickax.

The blood-stained pickax on the floor.

CHAPTER IV

SIMULTANEOUSLY, Leonidas and Cassie and Dow thought of Jock.

This was no sight for thirteen-year-olds.

Jock must not see.

"Turn together," Leonidas formed the words with his lips. "Then shut the door quickly, Dow, before he can look."

They turned, and Dow slammed the door.

"Shall I call Dalton One Thousand, Emergency," Jock said, "or just Uncle Root's private office number?"

"Oh, Jock, you saw her!" Cassie said.

"Please, Gran, don't get upset!" Jock was very pale, but his voice was determinedly self-possessed. "I wouldn't have peeked if I'd known. But I did, and—and that sort of—of thing, well, it doesn't upset me anywhere near as much as it upsets you. I don't mean it isn't awful, but you should have seen father after that toboggan spill. Or mother, when she missed that jump at Placid. They looked loads worse."

He didn't quite succeed in reassuring his grandmother, but he reassured himself, which Leonidas decided was more important.

"Why, Gran," Jock went on, "you even looked worse the time you fell off the porch roof! Bill doesn't know who she is, Gran. That's Miss Medora Winthrop."

"I know," Leonidas said.

"How? Oh, I mentioned her red wig, didn't I?" Cassie said. "Bill, this is simply fiendish! No matter what people thought of Medora Winthrop, no one had any right to do that to her! And here, in your garage!"

Dow took her arm.

"Come along upstairs. I'll call the colonel, and—"

"No, I'd better," Cassie drew a long breath as she gently propelled Jock toward the stairs. "Because it's all his fault. I tried to talk him out of that pickax. I said that was going too far."

"Cassie," Leonidas said, "do I understand that that pickax belongs to the colonel?"

There was a certain sinister irony, he thought, in murdering a woman with a pickax belonging to the Chief of Police.

"Oh, no," Cassie said. "No!"

"But you said—"

"The pickax belongs to you," Cassie informed him. "You see, Rutherford had so many. Seven or eight. He just likes to buy things in hardware stores. All winter long, he's been buying things for your house. And last night, he picked things over, and brought them here. The snow shovels, and the garden tools, and that infernal pickax!"

Dow opened the kitchen door for her.

"And what Rutherford's going to say when I tell him she was killed with it," Cassie said unhappily, "I can't think! Oh, dear, I can't phone here, with all this *red!* I'll go in your study. Come along, Jock!"

Leonidas and Dow leaned against one of the red-topped work spaces, and looked at each other.

"I feel," Dow said, "as if I had been beaten with a rubber hose. There are no marks, but I know something's happened. Bill, this is pretty damn grim!"

Leonidas twirled his pince-nez, and concurred.

"Rutherford's ax," Dow said. "Your garage. My aunt."

He whistled a few minor notes.

"I've had no opportunity," Leonidas said, "to express—"

Dow cut him short with a wave of his hand.

"You don't need to say condoling things, Bill. I mean, this is perfectly frightful, and I'm just beginning to catch on to the fact that it's real, and she *is* down there, and I didn't dream it. But—well, you saw Cassie's reaction. She gasped, and then she thought of Jock, and then she thought of Rutherford and his ax. And if there'd been one single, kindly thing to be said about Aunt Medora, Cassie would have seized that opportunity to say it. You know that."

Leonidas nodded.

"But she couldn't," Dow continued. "There wasn't anything to say. And in all honesty, my reaction was what a pity it had to happen in your new house. I think I'd feel a lot worse if it was someone else's aunt. D'you think that's a terrible thing to say?"

"Some day," Leonidas said, "I will tell you my random impressions of my maternal grandfather, whom you rightly hung over the fireplace as a museum piece. Of all the grandfathers I have ever met, I can honestly admit he was the least attractive."

"I didn't like his mouth," Dow said. "Well, then you can understand, Bill. That woman's made my life miserable. She made mother's miserable. She's dandled that damn money of hers over my head since I was a baby and when she and I came to the parting of the ways over this house of yours, mother and I agreed that it was like being released from jail. Even while I was her heir, there wasn't ever a semblance of friendly relationship between us. She—"

He broke off as Cassie and Jock returned to the kitchen.

Cassie walked over to a chromium stool and plumped herself down on it without saying a single word. Without, in fact, even opening her mouth or making a sound.

Leonidas stopped twirling his pince-nez, and put them on.

He would have considered it less ominous if Cassie had floated across the red and gray kitchen on a broomstick, shrieking shrill curses and snarling sepulchral threats.

When Cassie was silent like that, something catastrophic had taken place.

Leonidas asked her in a calm voice what the matter was.

"I have never," Cassie said, "been more miserable and dejected. I feel worse about this than I do about Medora Winthrop. This is disastrous!"

"What did Rutherford say?" Dow asked.

"Rutherford isn't there. He's gone," Cassie said. "Into thin air. And there's just that horrid man Rossi. He's just been *waiting* for something like this. He'll call in reporters—not that they wouldn't come, anyway. But they won't get anything but Rossi's story. Think of the headlines, Bill! Just think of them! Can't you see those headlines?"

"Frankly," Leonidas said, "no, Cassie. What headlines?"

" 'Wealthy Eccentric Murdered with Dalton Police Chief's Pickax,' " Cassie said promptly. "Don't you see,

Rossi won't call it your pickax. He'll call it Rutherford's. Jock, what were the others we thought of?"

" 'Dalton Pickax Murder,' " Jock said. " 'Foul Play Suspected. Dalton Police Chief Admits Buying Pickaxes. Insert: Dalton Police Chief Whose Pickax Was Murder Weapon. Colonel Rutherford Carpenter Denies Aide's Accusation.' See, Bill? That's what Gran is driving at. All because of Uncle Root warning Feeny—"

"Wait, Cupcake," Dow said. "There's something tangible we can snatch at and ask about. Rutherford warned Feeny. He's that old desk sergeant at headquarters, isn't he? Used to be the cop on our street when I was a kid. All right. Now, what was Feeny warned?"

"You see, Feeny was being guarded—poor man, he's not very subtle," Cassie said, "but from this guarded, mysterious way Feeny spoke, anyone at his end would assume that Rutherford was at my house, or that I knew where Rutherford was, and was just calling for him. He didn't want to tell me where Rutherford really was because someone was listening, see? Feeny was being guarded."

"It sounds to me," Dow said, "as though you suspected Rutherford of being on a Secret Mission."

"That's it! And if we call and tell about Medora Winthrop, while Rutherford is away, then that horrid Rossi will take charge, and we simply cannot have him. It would be fatal."

"We've got to call someone," Leonidas pointed out. "We can't hinder justice, Cassie. We can't just leave her down there!"

Cassie sighed.

"You know why Rutherford took over the police, don't you? It wasn't from boredom or because he was retired and found it dull doing nothing. The new mayor put Rutherford in to clean up the force. And he did. But you see, Bill, Rutherford was never able to weed out Rossi."

"Rossi is of the old regime?"

"Yes. Rutherford's always disliked him, and lately he's got on the track of something. I don't know what. He's just barely hinted at it. Feeny knows—Feeny used to work for us, long ago, and I think that maybe Feeny was the one that started Rutherford on the track. And I think that Rutherford's tracking down something about Rossi right this minute, and he doesn't want a soul to know. And I think that Rossi was listening in the office when I called, and that's why Feeny was so guarded."

"If you'd said that at first, Gran," Jock said pensively, "I think you'd have saved a lot of explaining. Now you understand, don't you, Bill, about everything? Rossi's tried before to make Uncle Root look silly, but it's awfully hard to do that."

Leonidas nodded. Sometimes the colonel's curt,

booming monosyllables misled people into thinking him stupid, but they usually lived to regret their error.

"But here," Cassie said, "he really can make Rutherford look utterly absurd! This is Rossi's chance. People won't think much of a chief of police who puts axes around for murderers to find."

"But will Rossi know about the pickax?" Leonidas inquired.

"Will he know it's Rutherford's? Oh, of course! Rutherford showed those axes to everyone. Rossi'll call in the reporters, and then there'll be all the headlines about Rutherford, and then what Rutherford finds out about Rossi won't matter. People will just say it's sour grapes. So we can't call Rossi, or anyone. We can't."

"But, Cassie," Dow said, "you just can't dismiss all thoughts of the police like that, with a jaunty wave of your hand! We might conceivably wait till Rutherford comes back from wherever he's gone. Only we don't know where he's gone, or how long he intends to stay there. We've got to do something right now!"

"Oh, we're going to," Jock said. "We've settled that."

"Oh, you have, have you, Cupcake? What?"

Leonidas swallowed. He thought he knew what was coming.

"We're going to solve this ourselves!" Cassie said triumphantly.

Dow slid off the table top where he had been perched.

"So?" he said. "So?"

Cassie stopped him just as he picked up the red phone.

"Put that back, Dow! That's what I said, and that's what I mean! We're going to solve this."

Dow looked at her, and then he turned to Leonidas.

"Bill, we've already got ourselves into a hole, dallying around like this. Take her by the hand, will you, and talk turkey to her? The House Moderne has gone to her head. She's daft!"

"I am not!" Cassie retorted. "Heaven knows you won't be any help in solving anything, but Bill can. He's done it before. See?"

She waved her hand as though that settled every· thing.

"Cassie," Leonidas said. "Miss Winthrop was Dow's aunt. The pickax belonged to your brother. The garage is mine. The beach wagon was a gift of yours and Jock's. Don't you see, Cassie, in one way or another, we all figure in this. And it's just possible that not reporting it might be considered faintly suspicious. If it had been the mousy woman—"

Cassie dove at her opportunity.

"What mousy woman? You keep mentioning her but you never get down to facts. Bill," Cassie pointed her finger at him, "you might have fooled Dow with your talk of Maharajahs, but you can't fool me! Something was going on, this morning, on that train. Something that made you terribly suspicious. And," Cassie continued, with one eye on the pince-nez, which had just begun to swing, "and something happened here, too? Didn't it now?"

"Cassie," Dow said, "you are simply playing for time. You know it. Bill isn't going to be fooled by you—"

Cassie's piercing scream brought both Leonidas and Dow to their feet. Jock, who was acclimated to his grandmother's reception of startling ideas, merely looked at her questioningly.

"Dow," Cassie said excitedly, "think! Think of mousy women! You big goon, think!"

"I don't even know what you *mean* by a mousy woman, Cassie! I only know we've got to call the police. And we've got to call 'em now!"

"Dow, can't you see what's happened? Don't you see this is worse than we ever thought? A mousy woman! Of course, there'd be a mousy woman! Why didn't I think? Dow, we've been living in a fool's paradise! If someone asked you to name a woman who looked like a mouse, and scurried around like a mouse, and was generally gray, and wee, and cowering, and—what's the rest, Jock? You were learning that the other day."

"Sleekit and tim'rous," Jock said promptly.

"Who would you think of, Dow?" Cassie demanded.

"Who would you think of at once, you great, gangling goon!"

Dow's mouth opened, and his cigarette dropped from his fingers.

"Stop goggling!" Cassie said impatiently. "Who do you think of?"

"Swiss Chard!" Dow said in a strangled voice. "Swiss Chard!"

Cassie nodded complacently.

"Swiss Chard," she agreed. "Exactly. Swiss Chard. Wouldn't you, Jock?"

"Swiss Chard!" Dow said before Jock could answer. "God in his heaven, Swiss Chard!"

Leonidas leaned over and picked up the cigarette before it burned a hole in his red and gray linoleum.

Cassie and Dow and Jock continued to survey each other ecstatically and say "Swiss Chard! Swiss Chard! Swiss Chard!" at intervals. As though, Leonidas thought, they were pushcart peddlers hawking vegetables through the streets.

He put on his pince-nez and looked curiously at the trio.

For his part, he was at a loss to understand why the mere mention of an edible leaf-beet should compel three people to carry on in any such abandoned fashion.

He started to say as much, but Cassie gave him no chance.

"Swiss Chard, Bill! That's the answer."

"M'yes," Leonidas said. "I hear you, Cassie. Swiss Chard. To the initiate, Beta Vulgaris. Swiss Chard. Esteemed by many as a tasty and fitting food, no doubt. Personally, it recalls to my mind the herbivorous antics of Nebuchadnezzar. May I remind you that in my garage at this moment, there is an unmistakable body? Is this any time to run on about leaf-beet?"

"Who said anything about leaf-beet?" Cassie retorted. "Bill, tell us every single thing about this mousy woman! Was she on the train? Was she? Was she here, in this house? Tell us every single thing about her quick!"

"Cassie," Leonidas said, "I've been endeavoring to tell one person or another about that mousy woman since the crack of dawn today. I've made several stalwart and valiant attempts to tell you. But, at this point, I regret having mentioned the mousy woman. It was a moment of weakness. The scuttlings of that woman are nothing for us to consider at this juncture. Miss Winthrop's body, on the other hand, is."

Dow looked at him and sighed.

"We know it, Bill!" he said. "We're straining every sinew to prod important data out of you, and you've just chatted about leaf-beet and Nebuchadnezzar! Now, *tell* us about the mousy woman. Was she short, and gray, and mousy, with gray eyes, and gray hair, and gray clothes? She scuttles, or scurries, whichever you like best. Go on from there."

"On the train this morning," Leonidas said, "there was such a woman. But there are thousands like her strewn over the world. Your description might fit any one of them. Let us, therefore, call the police, before—"

"And she looked sort of bewildered, and frightened, and terrified to the core, didn't she, all at once?" Cassie asked. "As if she'd curl like a caterpillar and fall into a trembling little heap, any minute. Didn't she, Bill? She's looked like that, always, but actually she's got the strongest will of any woman I know. Stronger than Medora Winthrop's, but I don't think Medora knew it, do you, Dow? Medora always gave the orders, so she just naturally thought she was boss. But I sometimes have wondered—how long has she been with Medora?"

"Forever," Dow said. "When I was a puling infant, I remember seeing Swiss Chard scurrying in Medora's background, making lists and doing things up in brown paper packages. She's kept the brown paper industry booming— What did you say, Bill? Are you talking about leaf-beet again?"

"I asked you," Leonidas said, "if Swiss Chard were a person."

"Goodness, you're stupid!" Cassie shook her head. "Sometimes you catch onto things like a shot, and sometimes I think you're as thick as Cuff Murray. Bill,

Swiss Chard is— What's her name, Dow? I suppose she must have a name, though I'm sure I never heard it. Miss Chard. Miss Um Chard. No, I don't think I ever heard her real name. What did Medora call her?"

Dow grinned.

" 'Chard-come-here,' " he said. "Or, 'Chard-I-want.' Sometimes, 'Chard-Chard-where-*is*-she!' Mother always called her just Miss Chard, and in my less articulate days, I called her Smiss Chard, and Swiss Chard was the next step. She's certainly been with Medora for thirty years, anyway."

"I don't think," Jock said, "that Bill understands even yet. You see, Bill, Swiss Chard is Miss Winthrop's companion, and she's a mousy woman. And—"

"And for goodness' sakes," Cassie said, "get on with your story about her, Bill! Hurry up!"

"If I do," Leonidas said, "will you solemnly promise me not to interrupt till I'm through with the whole recital?"

"Yes, yes, yes, yes! But do get on! Delaying us," Cassie said indignantly, "with all this talk of leaf-beet. Hurry up, won't you?"

Beginning with the flight of the mousy woman along the corridor outside his drawing room, Leonidas at last told his story of what had happened on the train.

Both Dow and Cassie had to restrain themselves at the mention of the brown paper package, and their eyes nearly bulged out of their sockets when he matter-of-factly informed them of its contents.

Then he went on to the beautiful girl with the red curls.

"I can't help interrupting," Dow said when Leonidas reached the part of the planted lipstick in the corridor. "If ever a girl was—why, to insinuate for a moment that she—"

"Ssh, dear," Cassie said. "You're young, you know. You can't tell beans about women yet, dear. Oh, no, you can't! If you could, you'd never have got yourself involved with Estelle Otis's daughter, ever. You wouldn't have let Medora change her will. You're still putty, Dow. But Bill knows. If this girl was pulling the wool over your eyes, Bill knows it. Go on, Bill."

Leonidas went on.

"So," he concluded, "there was a hand sticking out under those gray blankets, and there was the lipstick on the floor. And then Miss Chard cracked me over the head with the butt of a revolver, and I pitched forward. It wasn't much of a blow, but at the same time, the train lurched, and my head hit against that iron thing. Now, Dow, can you add or subtract anything?"

Dow said he was flabbergasted.

"So that's what you meant, Bill, when you asked me where was the body! Why didn't you tell, right then and there?"

"Don't be silly!" Cassie said impatiently. "No one would have believed him. They'd just have thought he was rambling. Bill had wit enough to know that if people didn't start asking him questions about a body the minute he came to, then he could be sure that they hadn't found one. If they had, he'd probably be answering questions yet."

"But it was so," Dow argued. "It happened, Cassie! That was something he saw before he got knocked out!"

"Yes, but he had to tell about it afterwards," Cassie pointed out.

"Was Bill all alone when you found him?"

Dow nodded.

"Looking corpselike, himself. You see, Bill, I'd been hovering in your car, waiting for another chance to get at you— Somehow, telling you about this house was easy to think about when Cassie and I planned it. But when you stuck on those pince-nez and stared at me, I got cold feet. Every time."

"Did you see me leave my drawing room?" Leonidas asked.

"Yes, and I followed. But I had to wait for a porter to shift bags in the vestibule, and then I stepped aside to let people pass. When I got into the next car, there wasn't a trace of you. I decided you'd gone ahead to the coaches, so I kept going. I thought I'd lost you for good, when I hadn't caught a glimpse of you by Back

Bay. I was going back to hover in your corridor some more, and just as we pulled out, that drawing room door popped open and there you were on the floor. But there wasn't any trace of anyone else in there. You saw that for yourself when they hunted the pencil— You know, I never guessed the Maharajah was a fake!"

"You ought to hear him talk about his friend Dr. Livingston," Jock said. "That's pretty good, too."

Dow winced.

"I've met the doc. The druggist and I put up one of his headache powders, from an old recipe. Bill, who could have been under those blankets?"

"The girl, of course," Cassie said. "It's perfectly obvious, if her lipstick was on the floor. They had a tussle, and her bag dropped—now I wonder if last year's zippers weren't *really* better."

Even Jock was stuck on that jump.

"Better than what, Gran?"

"Why, you remember, dear. Last year's bags all had zippers, and they always caught and wouldn't open, and we had to perform surgical operations with scissors to get things out. This year, everything's just namby-pamby catches, and bags just burst open if you look at them unexpectedly. Anyway, it's obvious, Swiss Chard knocked the girl out. And—"

"Why?" Dow said. "Why would she knock out that beautiful creature?"

"Why," Cassie asked reasonably, "should she knock out Bill? But she did. And he looked dead. You said so yourself. And then the girl came to. She probably wasn't hit very hard, and she couldn't have been hurt much if she chatted a few minutes later with the conductor about getting the Carnavon train. And she and Swiss Chard hopped off at Back Bay."

"Now why would Swiss Chard knock her over the head one minute," Dow said, "and then hop off with her at Back Bay Station the next? It doesn't follow, Cassie."

"They wanted to avoid any embarrassing explanations about Bill," Cassie said. "You've got to admit that however they may have felt about each other previously, Bill certainly gave them a common bond. If Swiss Chard left both Bill and the girl stretched out on the floor, the girl would have told on Swiss Chard. Don't you think so, Bill?"

Leonidas nodded.

"I've no doubt," he said, "that the girl pointed out that angle. It was better to call a truce, and depart, which they did. I had more or less figured that out when Dow began ordering Carl to drive up unplowed streets, and my own house key fell out of his coat pocket."

"You poor man!" Cassie said. "Biffed by Swiss Chard, and bumped by snow plows, and then that business of Dow and the limousine— You know, Dow, if that limousine episode's your idea of subtlety, I begin to see how you got involved with Elsa Otis and her buck teeth! And then the shock of this house being different, and finding Swiss Chard wandering around your terrace in the arbor vitae, and then finding Medora Winthrop—"

"M'yes," Leonidas said gently. "Quite so. I wondered if you'd forgotten that, Cassie. We found her at approximately three o'clock. Remember? It is now four. So, if you will be good enough to move away from that phone—"

Cassie didn't budge.

"An hour," she said coolly, "and we've found out heaps during it. You can't say it hasn't been a very profitable hour, Bill! We know this was some sinister plot of Medora's, only it backfired. We know it was Rutherford's ax. We know Swiss Chard is mixed up in it somewhere— Bill," Cassie prodded him suddenly, "what time was she here? What time did you come here?"

"I arrived at nine-thirty," Leonidas said. "And I saw the mousy woman a few minutes later."

"What time did you leave?"

"I haven't," Leonidas said. "I'm still here, Cassie."

"You mean, you haven't left this house since you came? Oh! Take this!" Cassie thrust a red-backed grocery order tablet and a pencil into his hand. "Bill

Shakespeare, you get to work! You take this and write down every single thing that's happened since you got out of your cab this morning. Every single thing. Every person who's been here, and where you were and what you did every minute of the time! Hurry, Bill!"

There was nothing but desperate urgency in her voice.

"Cassie," Leonidas said, "I couldn't. Any number of people came here. I couldn't possibly make a chronological list, if that's what you mean."

"What he did doesn't matter, Cassie," Dow said. "We've got to check up on the key situation, and find out how many thousand people had access—"

"Particularly since noon, Bill," Cassie said. "Wasn't it just before noon, Dow, that we passed by the Dalton Auditorium?"

"What has that got to do with it, Cassie?" Dow said. "Can't you stick to one point long enough—"

"You goon!" Cassie said. "You two goons! Medora Winthrop was alive when we passed by the Dalton Auditorium just before noon! I saw her going in!"

"That's impossible," Dow said promptly. "You just saw someone with the same sort of hat, or coat. You couldn't have seen her. If Bill's been here all day—"

"I saw her," Cassie said. "I was just going to point her out to you, and your rear-tire chain snapped again. Remember? Right on the corner by the A. and P. And by the time you got it fixed, seeing Medora had slipped my mind. But she was alive, and going into the auditorium just before noon."

"Now look here, Cass," Dow said, "Bill says he came here at nine-thirty, and he's been here all day long! She simply couldn't have been going into the auditorium at noon! She couldn't have been alive then. That would mean that she'd been killed in this house since Bill came!"

"Yes, yes, yes!" Cassie said. "That's why I said he had to write everything down. My, but you are stupid!"

"How could she have been killed here, in this house," Dow demanded, "without Bill's knowing it? She must have been here since before he came. Of course she was. She must have been here since last night, or early this morning. Don't you think Bill would have known, if people were being murdered in his own house?"

"Bill," Cassie said, "what did you do from noon on, till we came?"

"I slept," Leonidas said slowly. "Upstairs in my own room, on my own spool bed. I slept there from a few minutes after twelve, after Estelle and that lady judge left, until you two started war-whooping and waked me up."

"There," Cassie said, "that settles it. 'Dalton Police Chief's Pickax Death Weapon in Slaying of Wealthy Eccentric. Insert: Police Chief's Intimate Friend, Leonidas Shakespeare-in-brackets Witherall, Who Claims to Have Slept During Brutal Murder.' "

Leonidas broke the little silence that followed.

"M'yes," he said. "M'yes. I have just been the recipient of a psychic message from my old friend the Maharajah. He says, picturesquely, 'He who is in the grasp of the cobra can smile at the lightning's forked tongue.' But before we smile to any extent, let us make several very prompt investigations. Cassie, you telephone Miss Winthrop's house, find out when she left it, and where her companion, Miss Chard, is at the moment. Can you do that?"

Cassie picked up the phone.

"Easy. I'll be Mrs. Bledsoe, the Christmas card woman. Medora always got Christmas cards from her."

"Not in March," Leonidas pointed out.

"Mrs. Bledsoe starts selling cards again the first day of January," Cassie said. "I'll ask if Miss Winthrop's appointment for noon slipped her mind. That's a good question, because appointments always slipped Medora's mind. Then I'll ask what time she left. Miss Winthrop's residence? Mrs. Bledsoe calling. No, Bledsoe. The card one. Can you tell me—"

It was a lengthy conversation, punctuated by bursts of frenzied spelling on Cassie's part.

"That butler," she said as she replaced the receiver, "ought to have one of those things on his ear. He's the deafest old haddock— She left with Miss Chard, Bill, on the eleven-thirty Birch Hill bus for Dalton Centre. He sounded very positive about it, and he ought to know. That bus stops right outside her door. She had it put in, just for her."

"The door?" Leonidas asked.

"No, the bus stop. She bought up all the stock in the bus company, and they had to put the stop in. Bill, she and Chard left together at eleven-thirty to go to that lecture-luncheon. They're both expected home for dinner. That means—"

"That Miss Chard is at large," Leonidas said. "M'yes. Cassie, call headquarters and ask Feeny outright if Rutherford really is on the track of something vital to the department's well being, and how long it's going to take, and when he'll return."

Cassie's eyes were shining when she hung up after her call to Feeny.

"Yes! He said, yes! And he didn't know how long, but probably not very. Rutherford is to call here the minute he returns. There, that's all settled. First of all we'd better find Swiss Chard—"

"Gran," Jock said, "Uncle Root is *not* going to like this. But I've just been thinking—suppose I hadn't come right here from school. Suppose I hadn't come yet. Would you have opened that door downstairs, Bill?"

Leonidas shook his head.

"That is a point which the Maharajah and I were just mulling over," he said. "How did you come, by bus?"

Jock looked sideways at his grandmother.

"I hopped a pung," he said. "But it was perfectly safe, Gran. Really. And I'm sure no one saw me under the blanket. Anyway, Uncle Rutherford didn't, and that's all that matters. I could go back to the Adamses, Gran. They wanted me to finish the boat tonight."

Cassie nodded vigorously. "I'll call Sally Adams and ask her if she could bear the thought of having you stay with Tim another night— Where can you say you've been since school?"

"If they happen to ask, I'll say I went to the library after swimming. I often do."

"Fine. Now, Dow'll bundle you up in a rug and take you out to the car, so nobody'll see you leaving here," Cassie said. "Dow can let you off at the Adamses' door, and you can say he gave you a lift. Be sure and remember, darling, you've just never been here this afternoon, at all! So Bill hasn't opened that door downstairs. And it can't be opened until you officially come. You won't have to stay away long, Jock. Now, your pajamas—"

Cassie finally settled the details of Jock's clean underwear and toothbrush, and he was bundled off.

"Poor lamb," Cassie said, as she and Leonidas watched Dow drive away. "He never wanted to do anything less. But it's best all around that he isn't here. He mustn't be mixed up in this, or his family will never leave him with me again. Well, when Rutherford gets back and calls, we'll call Jock, and—"

"Cuff," Leonidas said suddenly. "We'll get hold of Cuff and have him stay downstairs in the hall."

Cassie said that Cuff was on sick leave.

"He broke his wrist wrenching a fresh truck driver out of a truck."

"But a broken wrist won't matter," Leonidas said. "Cuff with two broken wrists is still an abler guard than any three men I know. The garage entrance isn't shoveled, I noticed."

"No. Jock particularly asked me not to have that or the driveway cleared," Cassie said, "because he thought you might walk around the house before you came in. And if you saw the door or the drive, you'd guess the surprise right off. He was jubilant because the snow backed so high against the door."

"And there are no windows in the garage, are there? I thought not," Leonidas said. "I couldn't remember any. And just that one inside door, where we stood. M'yes. If we plant Cuff in the hall by that adhesive-taped door— Did Dow put the tape back before he left with Jock? Good. With Cuff there, we can pro-

ceed to set out on this project with the assurance that
no matter how many people may have keys to this
house, not one of them will get past Cuff into the garage. Can you call him?"

"Yes. He has a room at my cleaning woman's. Bill,"
she paused with her hand on the receiver, "who else
came here that you know of, besides Estelle, and Hattie Round, and that brush man?"

"Just a deluded man," Leonidas said, "but he came
so many times, he seemed like an army. Wanted to
take my icebox away, and give me another. I didn't
know people bandied iceboxes from door to door,
Cassie!"

"Oh, it's that racket again!" Cassie said. "They try
to sell you a bigger and better one. Or make you give
yours for another. They do that to people in new
houses, and put in a rebuilt with new paint, and take
out your new one. I thought Rutherford had cleaned
that up. Oh, dear, it's Mrs. Tudbury's fault. All those
keys, I mean. We gave her one, and then she had a
couple made, and so on and so forth. But Cuff can
take care of things—"

The back-door chimes sounded, and at the same
time, the Campbells started to tinkle at the front door.

"What do you do in a case like this?" Leonidas
asked. "When you're alone, which do you answer
first?"

"The nearest, unless the phone starts to ring, too, and then I ignore all of them. You take the back door. I'll take the front. Use the talker, be sure! Nobody must come in!"

It occurred to Leonidas as he hurried to the back door that the talker had never been demonstrated, so he peeked out of the kitchen window.

The massive figure of Cuff Murray stood on the back step.

Leonidas swung open the door.

"Cuff! We were just going to call you— Come in!"

"Hiyah, Bill! Say, Bill, she's a peach! She's a wow! Say, I bet you picked her up in Gay Paree, huh?"

Leonidas stared at the barber-pole lipstick which Cuff was holding out to him.

"Where did you get that!" Leonidas didn't ask it as a question.

"Your wife dropped it just now— Hey, what's going on in there? You got a party, huh?"

A shrill excited babble had suddenly arisen in the house.

"Well, I'll duck," Cuff said, "and come back later, Bill, to meet the wife. Boy, she's a wow!"

"Cuff!" Leonidas grabbed his arm and hung onto it. "You stay here! Don't you leave—stand there! Don't let anyone go downstairs!"

He pushed Cuff towards the door to the boiler room as the babble grew to a din.

"Don't let anyone past you!" Leonidas said. "No one. Understand?"

Cassie appeared in the kitchen doorway, and was almost immediately shoved to one side by the jostling throng of women that surged behind her.

Leonidas thought he had never seen so many women.

Hastily, he put on his pince-nez.

But they were no mirage. The women were real, and their number was increasing.

Babbling excitedly, and wearing happy, expectant smiles, they invaded his kitchen and filled it, and spilled over into the dining room.

And there were still more. The dining room became a swirling backwater. The radio in the living room blasted at intervals as it was switched from station to station. Leonidas could hear joyful shouts and a grinding sound as his ladder in the study was set in motion. The Campbells kept coming and coming as people played with the front-door bell.

Instinctively, he looked up at the sound of a shower being turned on in the bathroom over his head.

"It's them." Cassie had squirmed through the crowd and was bellowing in his ear. "They're everywhere. All over. They didn't listen to the talker. Or me. They just opened the door and marched in—and they're still coming!"

"What *for?*" Leonidas yelled back at her. "Why?"

"Surprise," Cassie cupped her hands to her lips. "Surprise!"

Before Leonidas could answer, Cassie was carried away on a sudden, surging wave, which deposited in her place at his side an imposing woman in black, with a corsage of gardenias trailing down her left shoulder.

She started to speak, and magically the room was quiet.

"Mr. Witherall, I'm Mrs. Tudbury, the president of the Tuesday Club! We've all had so much to do with your home, we almost feel it's our very own. And when our dear Harriet Pomeroy Round," she waited for the little burst of murmured approbation to die down, "and our dear Mrs. Otis, too, told us that you had returned, we just couldn't resist giving you a surprise tea! We were going to have tea at the auditorium after our lecture-lunch, and then we just thought, what *fun* it would be to surprise you in your little haven. So we just whisked around, and came, along with our sandwiches and urns."

Leonidas bowed from the waist, and stifled the impulse to tell Mrs. Tudbury that he could do with a good urn.

"So here we are, all of us," Mrs. Tudbury said, "with your surprise tea! And while we're here, we want to take a final look at everything, from attic to cellar—"

"There isn't any attic," Estelle Otis said.

"Well, we won't quibble about that, will we?" Mrs. Tudbury's smile was on the acid side. "We want to take a last look at every inch, every teeny-weeny inch, of your haven. Come, girls!"

CHAPTER V

NO PIBROCH, Leonidas thought, could compare with the martial inspiration of Mrs. Tudbury's rousing "Come, girls!"

Babbling with renewed vigor, the girls, as Mrs. Tudbury fancifully termed them, charged.

Cassie Price fought her way back to Leonidas's side.

"Bill, this must stop! Bill, what are you laughing at?"

"For ever after in my mind," Leonidas told her weakly, "I shall refer to the girls of the Tuesday Club as 'Tudbury's Horse.'"

Cassie leaned against him and laughed till the tears rolled down her cheeks.

"Oh, Rutherford'll howl! That's better than his crack. He said if you yelled 'Hi-yo Silver,' half of 'em would whinny. Oh, Bill, quick! Save Cuff!"

Without quite resorting to actual violence, Cuff was managing to fend off with his good arm the horde who were bent on viewing the boiler room and the lower floor.

"Leonidas," Estelle Otis said irritably, "this fellow won't let us by!"

She never looked more like a sergeant-major of Light Horse, Leonidas thought, than she did in that hat with the upright plume.

"He says," a woman wearing a hat like a tea caddy pointed an indignant finger at Cuff, "he says you said we can't go past him! Why not? I'm dying to see the maid's room. It wasn't done last week. Hattie, he does look like Shakespeare, doesn't he?"

Judge Round said he certainly did, and added that she, too, yearned to see if Cassie had got yellow or pink downstairs.

"Dear lady," Leonidas smiled his best smile and assumed his blandest manner, "dear lady, I wish it were possible for you all to examine the—er—nether regions. I wish from the bottom of my heart that it were possible for you to do so. Unfortunately, it is not."

"Why?" Estelle demanded.

"Please, Mr. Shakespeare!" Judge Round said brightly. "Please, Mr. Shakespeare!"

Leonidas put on his pince-nez and cleared his throat impressively.

" 'O'er this portion of my castle's vast expanse,' " he recited blandly, " 'A dusky hood like yonder falcon's lies.' "

"The Bard!" Judge Round said.

Leonidas bowed to hide his smile. He had held generations of boys at Meredith's in check by quoting just such hastily invented lines at them. There was something about a quotation from Shakespeare, even spur-of-the-minute Shakespeare, that seemed to stop people in their tracks. Tudbury's Horse were not routed, by any means, but they were no longer charging at Cuff like recruits at bayonet practice.

"Who's he?" Estelle indicated Cuff. "Do I know him?"

Cassie, overhearing the question, thanked God for Cuff's florid taste in clothes. With a bright yellow polo coat over his green-and-white striped suit, Cuff bore little resemblance to the blue-uniformed arm of the law who had given Estelle a ticket several months before. It was a perfectly justifiable ticket, but Estelle had gone straight to Rutherford about it.

"I'm sure I know him," Estelle said. "Now, who is he? Where have I seen him?"

"Darling, I think you're mistaken," Cassie said swiftly. If Estelle remembered, and started asking why policemen barred the doors of Leonidas's house, that would be tragic. "I'm sure you don't know him, darling. He's a rubber from the Turkish Baths. For Men Only."

It wasn't as good as Leonidas's falcon, Cassie thought, but it held Estelle.

It also gave Leonidas further inspiration.

"Because of the fever to which I succumbed on my recent trip," he said, looking Estelle straight in the eye, "my old friend Dr. Livingston advised a manservant with some knowledge of—er—massage. Mrs. Price was good enough to employ this young man."

"Oh," Estelle said. "So you're going to have a houseman."

"Yes," Cassie said, "isn't it lucky I chose blue for that room. A man would feel silly in pink. Wouldn't you feel silly in pink?"

"Who, me?" Cuff looked puzzled. "Oh, I'm in the pink except the wrist, Mrs. Price, and that'll be okay day after tomorrow."

"He's been unpacking, you see," Cassie said, "and things are a mess, with all his paraphernalia. You know."

Somehow, with a lift of her eyebrow, Cassie managed to convey the impression that the entire lower floor was stuffed with objects that were neither fitting nor proper for the girls to see.

They looked disappointed, but they began to trickle away from the door. With the deftness of a sheep dog, Cassie started to herd them into the hall.

Leonidas lingered behind with Cuff.

"Listen, Cuff. In the garage downstairs is a body. There's been a murder here."

Cuff gave no indications of excitement or surprise. It was his habit to take things as they came, and sudden death was just one of those things.

"That so?" he said. "Gee, I see. That's why you didn't want 'em to go down, huh?"

"Not a soul," Leonidas said, "is to get past you. Not an inch."

"Oh, boy, ten!" Cuff said. "Ten."

"What?"

"Ten places. You're going to find out who done it, ain't you? Well, I make ten places on the list if I help solve a murder. Gee, nobody won't get by me with a tommy gun, Bill!"

"Cling," Leonidas said, "to that thought."

He turned from Cuff and glanced around the kitchen. There were a couple of women pulling out drawers and poking into cupboards, and someone was boiling water in one of the copper kettles. No doubt for the tea, Leonidas decided.

"We're going to have tea in the living room," the woman at the stove said. "Don't you think that's best? We brought paper cups, too, so you needn't worry about dishes. And you must go in, Mr. Witherall. The rest are simply dying to meet you! You don't really mind our dropping in like this, do you?"

"Dear lady," Leonidas said, "it is a pleasure. I am

honored. Are you sure you have enough water? May I not fill another kettle?"

With infinite gallantry, he filled another kettle and set it on the stove.

Cuff watched him curiously from the door. Sometimes it seemed to him that Bill did the craziest things. But Bill usually knew what he was doing, and ten places were ten places. Cuff decided not to make the comment he had intended to make.

Cassie was not so reticent.

Steering Leonidas away from the stove, she backed him into a corner of the dining room and expressed herself thoroughly.

"Bill, you've bowled them over, and you can eat out for the next year on the strength of all this bowing and scraping, but if you don't stop, they'll just never leave! And we've got to get them out of here! Will you stop being so damned charming, and think of a way out? For the love of heaven, will you *do* something? Can't you throw a fit?"

"I am in constant communication," Leonidas said, "with my old friend Dr. Livingston, who advised against fits. They'd rush me to the hospital, Cassie, and where would we be then? So—"

"What's the matter with your voice?" Cassie asked suspiciously.

"I'm afraid," Leonidas said, "that I am on the verge of a severe bout of fever. It requires absolute quiet, and my special pills—"

Cassie beamed. "I see! Will aspirin do?"

"But put them in a plain envelope," Leonidas said. "Estelle Otis is getting that scurrilous, skeptical look in her eye. Hurry, Cassie. Stand by."

He marched into the living room, and with a bow, accepted a cup of tea from the hand of Mrs. Tudbury. He sipped at it once, and nodded graciously at her inquiry regarding its strength.

A moment later, the babble had stopped.

The Tuesday Club, pale with horror to the last girl, stared down at the mulberry broadloom and at the prone figure of Leonidas.

Just the suspicion of a froth had appeared at the corner of his mouth, which was working in a manner later described by Mrs. Tudbury as hideous. Even Estelle Otis accepted that mouth-working as genuine, and it was. The combination of laundry soap from the kitchen sink and tea from the Tuesday Club urns, Leonidas thought, was enough to work the oral cavity of a bronze statue.

Cassie pushed breathlessly through the circle and knelt down beside him. Her agitation was not acting, either. It was real. Unable to find her own handbag, she had been forced to dash upstairs through the crowd to the medicine closet.

"Oh!" Cassie said. "He warned me, and I *tried* to warn you when you came, but you just barged right in without listening! It's that terrible Manila fever. Strikes without the slightest warning. Get me cold water, somebody, and rubber gloves from the kitchen. Quick. And stand back. He told me just what to do. I've got his pills right here in this envelope. And don't be afraid of the froth. It's perfectly all right unless it happens to touch you."

The circle instantly widened.

"Get a doctor!" Estelle said.

"At once," Mrs. Tudbury added. "Call Dr. Strauss at once!"

Cassie had been waiting for that, and she had an answer ready.

"No, Dr. Livingston is on his way," she said. "He's spending the night here, and he ought to be here any minute. We expected him on the five-two. Tropical fevers are his specialty." She drew on the rubber gloves that someone held out. "It's all this excitement. Excitement and noise. I was afraid it would be too much, but he said no."

"Did he really?" Mrs. Tudbury said. "He seemed so pleased, and so charming!"

"He thought it was dear of you to come," Cassie opened Leonidas's mouth and slipped an aspirin between his lips, which caused his mouth to work even more violently. "He was so pleased. He asked me if I thought you'd like him to lecture on his trip, and world conditions. He was nearly bombed, you know. That's half the reason for this fever. Noise makes it come back. Where's that water?"

Leonidas, who yearned to take the entire glass of water at one gulp, consoled himself with the thin trickle that Cassie poured between his teeth.

"It's close in here," Cassie said. "Open the terrace doors. Wide. He ought to have air."

Mindful of the Tuesday Club's reaction to drafts, Cassie had been cherishing those doors in her mind like a thirteenth trump. A good blast of frigid arctic air from the predicted cold wave ought to send the girls flying.

But the group just moved a little to one side.

"Fine! If we just leave those open—the poor man!" Cassie decided to try another tack. "He's going to be so terribly embarrassed when he comes to and learns that you've seen this!"

Everyone agreed that it was too bad, but no one seemed to have the slightest inclination to leave.

Cassie began to feel desperate.

"Where's that man?" Estelle Otis asked. "That

houseman person. Have him carry Leonidas upstairs."

"He must not be moved!" Cassie wondered how much longer she could continue. "It's practically fatal to move someone with Manila fever until after the first spasm has passed."

She knew perfectly well that the instant Cuff left that door, Estelle and the judge and the others would go romping downstairs. A strip of adhesive tape would be no barrier to Tudbury's Horse.

"Well, he'll certainly get pneumonia, if he lies there in that draft," Estelle said. "*I* think you should call a doctor. And a nurse. Not," she sniffed, "not someone from a Turkish Bath. A real nurse."

"My dear," Cassie said bravely, "Dr. Livingston is not a Doctor of Divinity. Dr. Livingston has a nurse. He—"

"Who's that?" Estelle pointed to the girl who had stepped through the terrace doors into the living room. "For goodness' sakes! Who is she?"

Cassie, in a flash, mentally ticked off the details of gray suit, red curls, smart suède bag, and decided it was *the* girl. The girl on the train. The one Dow raved about. And Cassie didn't blame him for raving. The girl was undeniably beautiful, and Cassie liked her at once. She also liked the detached way the girl stared back at Estelle and the rest, as if they were a rehabilitated slum.

Leonidas knew from the electric silence that something had happened. He raised his head, and for an instant the girl's eyes met his.

"Who *is* she, Cassie?" Estelle demanded in a stage whisper. "Don't you know her?"

"I," the girl said easily, smiling at Cassie, "am the nurse."

Cassie needed no more.

"Dr. Livingston's nurse!" she said. "I didn't recognize you without that cap. Mr. Witherall hoped you'd come, and I'm so glad you did. He's the Manila fever case, you know, and I've been at my wit's end."

That last, she thought, was nothing but God's truth.

Walking across the room, the girl knelt by Leonidas and looked at him gravely. Then she rose and shook her head.

"Ladies, I shall have to request you to leave at once. Dr. Livingston considers it very serious when the patient's color is apparently normal. Absolute quiet is imperative. At once, please!"

Miraculously, in less than five minutes, the last pocketbook had been found, and Tudbury's Horse had tiptoed away.

"With tea urns and sandwiches, like Arabs into the night!" Cassie said as she returned to the living room and started drawing the curtains. "All of them! You can get up, Bill. They won't come back. Was it soap?"

Leonidas gulped down a glass of water.

"Yes. Miss—er—"

"Horn," the girl said. "Leslie Horn."

"Mrs. Price," Leonidas said, "Miss Leslie Horn. Er —you two have a lot in common, I think. Your routing of Tudbury's Horse was masterly. And timely. We are delighted that you dropped in." He waved her toward the green leather chair. "You could not have picked a more propitious moment."

"I didn't pick it," the girl said. "I just couldn't take that cold another second. I was frozen to the bone. Look, can you tell me—"

"You are lovely," Cassie said. "They didn't exaggerate a bit. You and Dow will make a simply marvelous couple. He needs someone with spirit. Between you and me, all that boy needs is a push. Bill, aren't she and Dow going to make a marvelous couple? Here—come back!" She grabbed at the girl's arm. "You can't go now!"

The girl looked from Leonidas to Cassie.

"Manila fever!" she said. "Tea urns. Arabs. Slugberry's Horse! I'm going to make a marvelous couple. Well, maybe it's me. Maybe I'm all wrong. What is Manila fever?"

"Soap," Leonidas told her, "and tea. And now, my dear Miss Leslie Horn, sit down. It's very clever of you to throw us on the defensive and assume we're demented, but before you undertake to leave, you are going to provide us with a number of explanations. Why did you come here?"

"I told you, I was cold!"

"M'yes," Leonidas said blandly. "M'yes."

Walking over to the terrace doors, which Cassie had forgotten to close, he removed a fur coat dangling from the outside handle. Then he stepped out on the terrace ,and returned with an assortment of snow-crusted luggage.

"M'yes," he said again as he shut the doors and locked them. "Now, why did you come here? What are you doing here?"

"Well, I'm—er— I'm hunting my Aunt Medora—"

"You're hunting your Aunt Medora?" Cassie and Leonidas spoke in unison.

"My—er—aunt. Miss Medora Winthrop."

"Your aunt?" Cassie said. "Your aunt *who?*"

"Medora Winthrop. People said she'd be here."

Cassie opened her mouth.

For a moment, Leonidas thought she was going to let loose one of her piercing screams. He wouldn't have blamed her had she emitted a series of them. He fully intended to join in.

Then, abruptly, Cassie closed her mouth and turned to him.

"Why didn't she ring the doorbell, then?"

"That," Leonidas said, "is a point well taken. If you are hunting your Aunt Medora Winthrop, why do you lurk on my terrace in the snow?"

"Eavesdropping," Cassie chimed in. "She heard me mention a nurse, and she just grabbed her chance to get in. She could have rung a doorbell. Either one. Both."

"I am not," Leonidas continued swiftly, "experienced in the art of aunt-hunting, but I question your methods. If I had lost an aunt, and if I thought she might be in a given house, I should unhesitatingly ring doorbells and make polite and pointed inquiries. I should not lurk on snow-bound terraces, sneaking—"

"Who sneaked?" the girl demanded.

Leonidas took from his pocket the barber-pole lipstick which Cuff had given him just before Tudbury's Horse had charged the kitchen.

"From this," Leonidas said, "I can only conclude that you have done considerable sneaking over a period of time. It is your lipstick, is it not?"

"That damn bag! It popped again!" the girl said.

"Zippers were better," Cassie said. "On the whole. Zippers—"

"Cassie," Leonidas said firmly, "we are not very vitally concerned with zippers, on the whole or otherwise. Miss Horn, what have you been doing, sneaking around my house? Why do you employ such odd measures to seek your aunt?"

"Tell him, dear," Cassie said. "He'll just worm it out of you if you don't. All those boys, you know. Rutherford says if you can get to the root of a small boy, you can get to the root of anything. So don't make it hard. You were sweet to save us from Tudbury's Horse, but we're going to find out the rest. Just let down your hair, as Jock says— By the way, who does it? I adore those little curls."

"Emil, at Joseph's," the girl said. "But they're a nuisance. Hats spoil them."

Cassie nodded understandingly, and the girl nodded back.

The two clearly had much in common, Leonidas thought. After an acquaintance of ten minutes, they understood each other perfectly, and unless he held them in check, they would probably start to exchange views on stocking runs and French dressing.

And the girl's story, he felt sure, would be just as incredible as anything Cassie Price had ever been mixed up in.

"Miss Horn," he said, "I asked you why you seek your aunt here, and why you go about it in such a quaint fashion."

"Well, really, I am hunting Aunt Medora, in a way. I mean—Aunt Medora. Well, in a way."

"Which, dear?" Cassie asked practically. "You're hunting her in a way, or she's your aunt in a way?"

"Both, sort of. She's a courtesy aunt. And if you want to know the bitter truth, I regret the day the relationship was ever brought up. Look, I've simply got to talk to someone about this! I've reached a point where things are too fantastic— What's that noise?"

"It sounds," Cassie said, "like fire engines. I'll go see."

After a brief conversation with someone at the front door, Cassie returned to the living room.

"It was the fire engines! And what do you suppose, Bill, they were coming in here! They had a call to put out a fire in the cellar of Forty Birch Hill Road, but of course it was Church Hill. Not Birch Hill. I told Dever to hurry right over to Forty Church Hill before they burned up. Go on—do people call you Leslie? Go on, Leslie."

"Well, I've got to find things out. I'm worried, even now."

"I knew it," Cassie said, "the minute you came through the door. You looked harassed. Just as I was. Tell us about it, dear. Or do you want to dig out something special before she begins, Bill?"

Leonidas didn't even hear her. He was too busy considering the fire engines which Cassie had dismissed so casually as a mistake. He felt sure they weren't. Someone had sent them to his house, and specifically to his cellar.

Someone wanted Miss Medora Winthrop's body to be found.

Cassie repeated her question.

"As long," Leonidas swung his pince-nez, "as some few items are explained to my satisfaction, I don't care where Miss Horn begins. Er—at the train, perhaps?"

Leslie Horn bit her lip.

"I'm truly ashamed of leaving you there, like that. But—oh, I don't know where to start! I'm an artist. A commercial artist—"

"Are you married," Cassie asked interestedly, "or engaged, or anything like that? No? That's nice. He's momentarily engaged, but Elsa doesn't matter. You can't even call her a wild oat. Where is Dow, Bill? He ought to have been back hours ago— D'you suppose something's happened?"

"Something," Leonidas assured her politely, "will happen to you if you don't let her do the talking, Cassie. All right, Miss Horn. You're a commercial artist; Medora Winthrop was your aunt in a way, and you're hunting her in a way, and someone said she'd be here."

"Yes. Well—look, I've got to begin a year back. It sounds silly, but I have to."

"Isn't it amazing," Cassie said, "when you start to explain something, how far back you have to go? Take the Manila fever. That began when Bill decided to build a gabled cottage, and it turned out to be this house. That's why he ate soap—"

"Cassie!" Leonidas said.

The girl drew a long breath.

"Look, a year ago I did some illustrations for a story in *Women's Talk*, and they had a snapshot of me and the author on a back page. And later, Medora Winthrop wrote and asked me if I were the daughter of her old friend Leslie Flagg who married Robert Horn, because I looked like her, and she'd had a daughter named Leslie. And if I were, she used to dandle me on her knee."

"And you were, of course," Cassie said.

"Yes. So I wrote her back, and then there were a lot more letters, and then some talk of a visit here crept in, and finally she set a date, and sent me tickets. To make a long story short, I came over on the midnight from New York, the night before last, and came out here to Dalton yesterday morning."

"Yesterday?" Cassie said. "But I thought it was *this* morning. You mean, this morning, don't you?"

The girl sighed.

"Both. I've practically lived on one train or another

since the night before last. Yesterday morning I came here to Dalton, and Medora's, and after five minutes in Medora Winthrop's house, I realized that I'd made a grave error."

"You judged her from her handwriting, didn't you?" Cassie said. "I thought so. It was so neat and delicate. You'd never guess from that writing what an old harridan she was."

Leslie Horn nodded as she studied the Sargent over the fireplace.

"Yes, it was. I couldn't remember her dandling me, naturally, but I had visions of someone who looked like my mother and lived in a neat white house with apple trees, and a cat by the fireside. And I landed in that awful household! Why, before I had my hat off, Aunt Medora—that's how she signed her letters—was throwing clocks at the butler— Look, d'you hear those fire engines again?"

Cassie went to the front window.

"For heaven's sakes. I *told* Dever he made a mistake. He can see for himself we've got no fire—" Cassie stopped short, and blinked.

"Someone's playing a practical joke," Leonidas said. "Tell them so. Convince them. Add that I am ill with Manila fever."

The girl looked curiously at Leonidas as Cassie bustled out of the room.

"Why," he gave her no opportunity to ask questions, "why did she throw clocks at the butler?"

"I don't know. Nobody seemed to think it was unusual."

"Was there any specific purpose to this visit?"

"No, it was just the result of all those letters. From now on," she added, "I curb my correspondence. No more folksy letters to strangers, even if they fed me prune juice. I've learned a mighty lesson."

Leonidas thought to himself that she had barely read the preface.

"Dever's terribly sorry," Cassie came back. "He says if there's another call, they'll try to trace it. Leslie, if you were here yesterday, when did you get back to New York to take the midnight last night? I'm awfully confused."

"Well, after lunch yesterday Chard went shopping, and Medora went to take a nap, to rest up for the tea party she was throwing for me. Then the phone rang, and that butler passed it six times without noticing. So I answered, and it was my agent calling. He had a swell job for me, but I had to be in his New York office by six to see people about it. So I grabbed my bags and stuff, which I hadn't unpacked, and dashed off a note, and caught that foul bus. I didn't have time to wake Aunt Medora and explain, even if I'd wanted to. Then I took a cab from the village to Boston, and got a plane to New York. I know it wasn't proper to rush away like that, but I'd had my fill of Miss Medora Winthrop, the old dandler!"

"Very wise of you, dear," Cassie said. "What prompted you to come back?"

Leslie Horn said feelingly that she wished she knew.

"Anyway, I got the job, and had dinner and went to the movies, and then I went back to my apartment. And there in the entrance hall stood Chard—"

"Chard? What was she doing there?" Leonidas demanded.

"She was so excited, it was hard for me to get the jist of things. Seemed she'd taken a plane over after me, and she wanted me to come back at once, by plane, with her."

"Why?"

Leslie Horn lighted a cigarette.

"It was all so frenzied, I never thought till later that Chard hadn't actually given me any reason. I got the impression that Medora'd been taken ill, and wanted me, though I must admit Chard didn't say so. And they'd never found my note. I'd told the butler about it—"

"But the deaf old thing never understood you, of course," Cassie said.

"Apparently not. Anyway, the snowstorm grounded the plane Chard planned to take, so we took the midnight instead. And I still thought I was being noble, and going on an errand of mercy to mother's old friend, until I waked up in the night and found Chard going through my pocketbook, and fingering the hundred-dollar bill I'd got from my agent as an advance."

"What?" Cassie didn't exactly scream, but the effect was the same. "What did you do?"

"Told her coldly she had my pocketbook by mistake, and she dropped it like a hot cake, and looked so completely terrified I didn't pursue the subject. I felt sorry for her. Some people pry, without meaning any harm, and I decided she was just a prying, meddlesome little thing. So I went back to sleep. I thought I'd·squelched her. But when I woke up later, around dawn, she was gone. And I discovered she'd been in my briefcase, and taken—"

"The gun and the handcuffs," Leonidas said gently. "M'yes."

"How did you know?"

"I saw them. Er—why a gun, and handcuffs?"

"I don't know," Leslie said. "I don't know what goes on in the mind of a mouth-wash and tooth-paste company! All I know is that they're willing to pay me handsomely for a picture of a gun and a pair of handcuffs against a background of spring flowers."

Leslie tossed her half-smoked cigarette into the fireplace.

"They'd given me that gun and the handcuffs for models," she went on, "and I couldn't afford to have anyone swipe 'em. I didn't intend anyone should. So I dressed and waited for Chard to come back. I knew she'd have to, because all her clothes and things were there. And when she scuttled in, I grabbed her and shook her till her teeth clattered. I had to threaten her with every known form of torture before she finally broke down and told me that she'd wrapped up the gun and the handcuffs and thrown 'em away! And just as I started for the water cooler, she stopped blubbering long enough to announce that Shakespeare saw her do it. At that point, I decided that the woman wasn't just a harmless, meddlesome busybody. I decided she was stark mad."

"M'yes. Let us," Leonidas said, "hear the rest."

"Suddenly," Leslie said, "I began to realize that Chard had given me no real reason for rushing back to Dalton. I didn't really know Medora was sick. There was no telling what Chard might be up to. I began to get worried. Then I thought, suppose someone really saw her throw that package away, and had picked it up—after all, a gun and handcuffs aren't things you can explain in any offhand manner. I'd taken them for granted. They were models. But someone else might look on them very differently."

"M'yes," Leonidas said. "They are not standard accessories for the average young woman. So that's why you planted the lipstick, and arranged the lipstick hunt?"

"I *had* to get that package. I couldn't go back and tell old Blotz that I'd lost his gun and handcuffs. He'd give the job to someone else. And I didn't want to have to try to explain to a lot of cops. Of course, the gun wasn't loaded, and the handcuffs were locked, and I didn't have the key. But even so!"

Leonidas nodded.

"I noticed that they were quite harmless, but, as you say, even so."

"Shakespeare, you did look! You took it out, and looked, and put it back before I came! Oh, I should have known! I wondered about you. You were so bland. But when you didn't say anything, or follow me, I thought I was just imagining things. And I thought that maybe I'd been harsh on Chard. After all, you do look like Shakespeare. Anyway, I took the package, and walked to the club car, and then back to our drawing room, and—"

"And Chard hit you over the head!" Cassie said. "We guessed that. Bill's marvelous at figuring things out. Go on, dear. She hit you. How did you *ever* let that happen?"

"I never expected it! I told you, after I saw Shakespeare, I thought I'd misjudged Chard. I thought she was just meddlesome, and queer. And after I'd shaken her teeth out, and threatened her to boot, I never suspected that she'd up and biff me with the heel of a ground gripper shoe!"

"Why should she?" Cassie demanded.

"I suppose it was the only thing she had at hand. Oh, you mean why she hit me? I don't know. I don't know why she tried to dispose of my gun and handcuffs. And when I came to, there were you," she pointed to Leonidas, "looking as dead as a man can look. And there was Chard, blubbering away, with a gun in her hand. First I thought she'd shot you, and then I realized she couldn't have, because it was my model gun—apparently, after she knocked me out, she'd taken the gun from the brown paper package in my bag."

"Dislodging, in the process," Leonidas said, "your ubiquitous lipstick, which rolled on the floor and lured me in the drawing room. Did Miss Chard offer no explanations?"

The girl shook her head.

"She was in no state to think. Neither was I. I only knew if we called anyone in, and they looked at you, and the gun and handcuffs, Chard and I would share a cell. And I'd never get the gun and handcuffs back. I felt Chard was crazy, but I couldn't figure out what she was up to. If she were a kidnaper, or something sinister, she wouldn't have been blubbering around, waving that useless gun. She'd be giving orders in a sharp voice—"

"Sharp, staccato voice," Cassie corrected. "That's the way Lieutenant Haseltine does. Do you know him, by the way? This sounds like one of Haseltine's adventures."

Leslie Horn laughed.

"I did a jacket for one of those books last year, and I was so enchanted, I read straight through the set. Frankly, I've thought of Haseltine more than once in the last day or so. Anyway, you see my point. If Chard were a sinister creature, at work on a sinister plot, she'd either have been giving orders behind a bona fide gun, or she'd have beat it. I knew by then that you were alive, Shakespeare. I saw your bump, and you were breathing. And I knew it would almost be worse, if you came to and started a ruckus. I shook Chard and told her to snap out of it, that you were alive, and we had to get out, and she had to do some quick thinking. And d'you know, she did!"

"Oh, she would!" Cassie said. "You'd never guess how efficient she is, under that scared manner. I know. I've been on committees with her. It was she who thought of the Carnavon train, and making the conductor and everyone think you'd been out of your drawing room for a long time, so they'd figure Bill got bumped when that snow plow got in the way. Chard thought of that, didn't she? And then you dashed off the train at Back Bay— Go on from there."

"Yes." Leslie's voice seemed strained. "Yes. She made it, but I dropped my pocketbook, and of course the catch popped. And while I picked things out of a snow bank, that Carnavon train went puffing off without me."

"But you weren't really going with her!" Cassie said.

"Yes, I decided that any existing plan would be pretty well rooked by this quick train change. And Chard had already gummed things up when she biffed Shakespeare— That reminds me, Shakespeare. She didn't think you saw her hit you, and she said even if you had, probably no one would believe you if you told them."

"I did see her face," Leonidas said, "but her theorizing was absolutely correct. I wonder how she—m'yes. So Miss Chard planned all that hasty exiting at Back Bay, but you still felt that she was not the master mind behind this strange expedition of yours?"

"Look," Leslie said, "she didn't want to get mixed up with the authorities, but she didn't want to involve me, either. Otherwise she'd have yelled for help, there in the drawing room, and pointed to you, Shakespeare, and said I was responsible. She could have. In this whole mess, it's her word against mine. And the word of Miss Medora Winthrop's companion is as good as mine. But she didn't take any steps. The only thing she seemed to have on her mind was getting me to Dalton. And while we waited there in the day-coach vestibule, before we got into Back Bay, she muttered something about doing her duty, and fulfilling her obligations. And that led me to believe that if there was dirty work afoot, Medora Winthrop was responsible."

"We thought that," Cassie said. "So you decided to find out?"

"Yes. I changed my mind for the millionth time, and decided that Medora was the crazy one. Not Chard. Poor, frightened little Chard was trying to carry out Medora's orders, and all this biffing, and throwing away of the gun and handcuffs, was just sheer panic. Then, after I picked up the things that had fallen from my pocketbook, I came to. Poor, dear, frightened little Chard had swiped my hundred-dollar bill from the inside compartment of my bag."

Leonidas and Cassie both blinked.

"Chard took it?" Cassie said. "Chard?"

"It couldn't have dropped out. The compartment was still snapped. She took it while I dashed out and palavered about trains with the conductor. While she was getting dressed. That left me with fifteen cents to my name. And I discovered that she'd also made off with my brush box—you know, one of those long, tin boxes. And the gun and handcuffs, too."

"Not even the estimable Haseltine," Leonidas said, "ever achieved anything quite like this. His adventures have been more violent, but certainly no more puzzling. What did you do then?"

"Hocked my watch, and took the next train to Dalton— Tell me, how many varieties of Dalton are there?"

"Fifteen," Leonidas said.

"Seventeen," Cassie corrected him. "East Dalton, West Dalton, North Dalton, South Dalton, Dalton Hills, Dalton Farms, Dalton Centre, Dalton Village, Dalton Falls, Dalton Upper Falls, Dalton Lower Falls, Daltondale, Daltonville, Daltonham, Dalton Landing, Daltonwood—how many is that?"

"Enough," Leonidas said. "Do I gather that you got to the wrong Dalton, Miss Horn?"

"I got to more wrong Daltons that I would have believed possible. I got to them," Leslie said wearily, "on busses, trains, streetcars—once I even took a subway to a ferry."

Leonidas chuckled.

"Dalton the Garden City," he said, "is easily accessible. It tells you all about it in the Chamber of Commerce booklets. When did you arrive at Birch Hill?"

"At twelve o'clock, on that bus, with a dime left. That butler said that Miss Winthrop and Miss Chard were out, and would be back for dinner, so I said I'd wait. I hadn't the capital to set out and track them down."

Leonidas nodded thoughtfully. Cassie had seen Miss Winthrop shortly before twelve. Leslie Horn arrived at twelve. Sometime between twelve and quarter past two, or thereabouts, Medora Winthrop had been killed in his garage.

Cassie's question echoed his thoughts.

"And did you just stay there and wait, all afternoon, Leslie?"

"Oh, no. I went out and walked till I got too cold to walk any more, and then I went in and sat till I couldn't endure being watched any more—"

"Watched? Who watched you?"

"Oh, practically everyone. They took turns. Butler, maids, cook. Just stood and gaped at me. I delicately brought up the topic of food, but nothing came of it, and I was virtually famished when someone named Bledsoe telephoned— What did you say?"

"I choked," Cassie said. "Go on."

"Well, while Bledsoe and the butler and the cook had a field day discussing Christmas cards, I slipped into the library to see if there wasn't an old peppermint or something left to munch on in the box of candy I'd brought Medora yesterday—and *what* do you think?"

"What?" Leonidas asked obediently.

"On the library desk," Leslie said, "sat my hundred-dollar bill! And my brush box! And the gun and the handcuffs! I grabbed 'em, and grabbed the rest of my things from the hall, and I just got the hell out of that house as fast as I could. Just missing a bus, too. It was turning the corner."

"Which bus?" Leonidas asked. "What time?"

"The four-thirty. Then I walked over here, intending to ask someone to phone for a cab. I had no desire to go back to Medora's, and I could afford a cab again. I was fascinated by this house, anyway. I walked around here a couple of times during the afternoon, and wished I could see the inside."

"You are unique," Leonidas said. "Everyone else has. And that, I gather, was when you saw Cuff, and ran away, and dropped the lipstick. Why on earth did you tell him you were my wife?"

"I never did! I ran then, because I'd just seen you, of *all* people! You passed by a window. And then I saw all those cars, and those women trooping in, and I heard one call and ask another whose car Medora Winthrop was in. And I decided that it might be fun to confront Medora and Chard, and you, and see what the reactions might be. So I waited on the terrace.

And then I simply couldn't resist being the nurse. I knew you'd welcome one, from what you said, and I was really getting terribly cold."

"And?" Leonidas prompted.

"And I wondered why you were putting on the sick act. And I wanted to find out what part you played in all this. And I still do. Shakespeare, stop swinging those damned glasses, and looking at me like that! I told you before I began that it was fantastic. Here." She opened her pocketbook. "Here's the bill. Here's the gun and the handcuffs. The brush box is in my briefcase, over in the corner. Now, can you make any sense of any of it?"

"Of course not, dear," Cassie said. "Except that Medora had a plot, and it backfired. When did you eat last?"

"I've forgotten. Look, why was I rushed back here? Why was Chard so anxious for me to come back to Dalton? Why did she swipe those things? What's behind it all? Last night, Chard had a plane waiting to fly me back to Medora. This afternoon, she and Medora go to a club, having apparently dismissed me from their minds. What was I wanted for? What was I supposed to do? The whole thing appals me. I'm still worried!"

"Well, it's no more fantastic than our story," Cassie said consolingly. "I shouldn't believe a word of yours, if it didn't tally in parts with Bill's. You wouldn't believe ours if you hadn't seen her all sprawled—"

Cassie stopped short.

"Oh, yes, I would!" Leslie Horn said. "You've spoken of Medora in the past tense ever since her name was uttered. D'you think I'd have gone into such detail otherwise? I assumed she was dead. But— look, have I fallen into a plot, after all? Have I?"

"Don't you worry, dear," Cassie said. "It's hideous she had to be killed here, with you wandering around and Bill upstairs, and my brother's pickax. But just don't let it worry you. You can't honestly admit to any deep personal grief, and Bill's going to settle everything. His mind is a dynamo, you know. Now, come out to the kitchen, and get some food, and then we'll set right out and find Chard—Leslie, when *did* you eat last, dear?"

"This morning some time. A bus driver divided his lunch with me at the end of a line— Look, *what*—"

"Eat first." Cassie propelled her toward the kitchen. "We all need food. Come, Bill. I've been perishing with hunger since Tudbury's Horse—"

But Leonidas lingered behind in the living room. It was not yet six o'clock, he noticed, although it seemed to him that a month or more had elapsed since six that morning, when he walked out into that train corridor and into all this perplexing, thwarting muddle.

Cassie could lightly refer to his mind as a dynamo, but it was a dynamo in the throes of sabotage. The fate which so constantly pursued and buffeted Lieutenant Haseltine was more turbulent, and obstreperous, and sensational, but it was not a whit less exasperating. The dashing young officer had never been thwarted like this.

All day long, Leonidas thought, he had been interfered with, frustrated, thwarted. He entered a commonplace Pullman drawing room, and was promptly cracked on the head. He tried to get to his new house, and was foiled by unfinished streets and snow drifts. He tried to enter his own home, and was stopped by a policeman. He tried to see his house, and his explorations were nipped in the bud by brush men and Welcoming Committees and icebox racketeers. He tried to rest in his new house, and a woman was murdered at once in his garage. And before he had a chance to think why, Women's Clubs came to tea. Fire engines called. And a beautiful girl earnestly told him a story that even Lieutenant Haseltine would blush at.

Leonidas sighed.

Then he sat back in his chair and slowly swung his pince-nez.

If Leslie Horn's story were true, the only conclusion

he could draw was absurd, too absurd to waste time brooding about until Miss Chard was found, and forced to fill in the gaps.

His own day, now that he considered it, led him to equally absurd conclusions. The brush man was genuine, but the refrigerator man— Cuff might know about that, possibly.

Leonidas half started to go into the kitchen and ask, and then he sat back heavily in his chair again.

The thought which had come to him out of the blue was so alarming that it stunned him. He closed his eyes and tried to think it out.

Tudbury's Horse had admittedly come on the spur of the moment, but suppose that someone had deliberately applied the spur? Anyone who wanted the body of Medora Winthrop brought publicly to light could reasonably assume that Tudbury's Horse would find her.

Leonidas toyed with the idea, and found it sound.

But, when that mad tea party came to an end, why had the police not been summoned? Why had the Fire Department been called? What was the reason for all this beating about the bush? Why was someone trying to harry them? What was going to happen next?

"Exactly!" Leonidas murmured to himself. "M'yes. What, indeed?"

That was it, of course. Someone felt sufficiently safe and sure of themselves to want the body found. Someone was purposely harrying them. It was a part of the plan.

At last, Leonidas thought with satisfaction, the dynamo was turning, even if it turned in the wrong direction. At least it was whirling. It was all right for Lieutenant Haseltine to do his best thinking in a turmoil of action and crowds, in whizzing cars, or in rocket ships, or while misinformed mobs howled for his lifeblood. That was all right for fiction.

In fact, it was better to sit alone, in solitude, in isolation, and just think quietly.

Leonidas smiled, and opened his eyes.

The smile froze on his face.

CHAPTER VI

HE WAS not sitting alone in solitude, or isolation, or anything remotely resembling either state.

Quietly squatting on his mulberry broadloom carpet, surrounding his chair, backed up almost into the fireplace, were a quantity of little girls. Dozens of little girls. Red-cheeked, bright-eyed little girls who were studying him with that inquisitive, slightly suspicious intensity peculiar to the very young.

Leonidas stared unblinkingly back at them, confident that the mirage would evaporate. Of course, the little girls were a mirage. They had to be. Hordes of small girls couldn't permeate a room so quietly in such a short time. They were a mirage. A myopic error. A vision conjured by a tired mind.

He became aware suddenly of a woman looming in the doorway.

"I can't imagine," Judge Round said absently, ignoring Leonidas, "what became of Wendy—"

And forthwith, she departed.

Leonidas hastily whipped on his pince-nez. There

was an aura of Thurston and Houdini in the way the judge vanished from sight.

"All," Leonidas told himself firmly, "a bad dream. Myopic errors."

He closed his eyes for a moment, and then opened them again.

There was no sign of the judge, but the little girls were still there. They were real.

Unlike Tudbury's Horse, they seemed to have no conversational bouquets poised to fling at him. They appeared to be quite comfortably content to sit and stare without any explanatory verbiage whatsoever. If, their expressions said, if you want ice broken, you go right ahead and break it.

"Er— Good evening," Leonidas said.

He took off his pince-nez, and then tentatively put them on again.

Several of the little girls giggled.

"In the outermost reaches of far Mongoon," Leonidas remarked, "which, incidentally, is ruled by my good friend the Maharajah, I understand that there is an Upper Urdul tribe called the Mimballa, whose womenfolk take the vow of perpetual silence, or Mimball. Am I right in thinking that you are Mimballa from the Upper Urdul?"

All of the little girls giggled, and the two nearest him squealed.

"We're from Dalton *Centre!*" one of the pair said.

"Oh! that's a pity," Leonidas said. "And you're not Mimballa, either?"

"We're Pussycats!"

"M'yes. Of course. To be sure." Leonidas never batted an eyelid. "You'd have to be, to creep in here so quietly. Will you be stopping long, d'you think, or will the catnip trail beckon again? I mean, I've only got beds for four."

The little girls broke down completely.

"You're funnier than he said!" the small blonde spokesman announced.

"Er—who?"

"Jock!"

"Ah, yes. Jock. You know Jock?"

"He takes my sister to the Friday Afternoon Junior Assemblies. He thinks Sis is keen." Everybody had a good giggle at that. "Did you like his surprise?"

"I haven't seen it," Leonidas said, quickly. "Jock hasn't been here to show it to me."

"He hasn't? I guess he doesn't know you're home," the blonde child said. "I'll have Sis phone him, when I get home."

At least, Leonidas thought, the infant had a home, and gave some indication of returning to it, which was more than could be said for any member of Tudbury's Horse.

"Sis likes to phone him. She thinks up things to ask him, and then she calls him, and then Mum has a fit. Mum had a fit about this house, too."

"Did she," Leonidas said, "indeed?"

"Yes. Mum says it's awful the way everyone's made a camp ground out of it. She was talking with Judge Round just before we left—"

Leonidas was about to make a tentative inquiry regarding Judge Round's part in the expedition when Cassie spoke from the doorway.

"For the love of heaven! Bill, where did they come from?"

"I don't know," Leonidas said honestly, "but I don't feel that they intend to curl up on the hearth forever. Er—they claim," he added, "to be Pussycats. I thought I saw Judge Round, but—"

"Elsa's work," Cassie said. "You're that Sunday School class of hers, aren't you? Or the small scouts, or something? Didn't Elsa Otis bring you here?"

"Well," the blonde child said, "no. Not all of us. It was Judge Round. And Elsa, too. You see, Geraldine couldn't help Elsa bring us, so the judge did. She helped bring us here."

"A kindly gesture," Leonidas said, dismissing the base suspicion that had entered his mind. "Er—why? Why—er—here?"

"Because the sleighs hadn't come, and it was cold on

the corner. See? So the judge thought we'd better wait here. So she told us to come in quietly so we wouldn't disturb you. We just came on the bus, and we're going to Bradley's Farm for supper. In two sleighs."

"Are you," Cassie demanded, "the one who phones?"

"No, I'm the one-that-phone's sister—here she is!"

Elsa Otis, having stomped the snow from her ski boots all over the hall, clumped into the living room, peered through her shell-rimmed glasses at Leonidas and Cassie, and displayed her very toothy smile.

"Oh, hello, Mr. Witherall," she said. "I didn't know you were home." Clearly it would have made no difference to her if she had. "Do you like your house?"

"Yes," Leonidas said. Elsa, he thought, was not just a miniature of her mother. She was living proof of his conviction that stout girls should not wear pants. "Yes. I like it. Er—do you?"

"I think the linen closet is lovely," Elsa said. "I think that linen closet is simply divine. Of course, the rest is quite nice, too. I mean if you like modern. As mother said, it's all right if you *like* modern."

"I suppose," Cassie remarked acidly, "the two of you would prefer something with a thatched roof and an earthen floor, and—"

Leonidas stopped her before she had a chance to get going on the topic of tallow candles and open plumbing.

"Er—Elsa," he said, "before you depart for your sleighs, may I have—"

The judge loomed again in the doorway. With her was a small, pigtailed girl, and a short, timid, little man who looked more like Caspar Milquetoast than anyone Leonidas had ever seen.

"I found Wendy," Judge Round said. "She was sliding. She—"

"Er—not sliding," the little man interrupted timidly, "building a snow man, dear."

"I've explained to her," Judge Round continued, "the obligations one has to one's group. She won't slide again. Are you feeling better, Mr. Witherall? I had the girlies come in quietly so you wouldn't be bothered. And before we go, I want the girlies to see Jock's little—"

"If you mean the surprise, he hasn't seen it," the blonde child said quickly. "Judge, *he* didn't take off his rubbers."

She pointed to the little man.

"Ernest," Judge Round said, "take off your rubbers. Really, Mr. Witherall, haven't you seen the surprise yet? That's odd."

"It's so cute," Elsa said, "can't we see it anyway, Cassie?"

"No," Leonidas said. "Before you depart for your sleighs, Elsa, may I have my key? Er—all keys? From now on, I expect there will be someone here to answer the bell when you call."

Elsa sniffed as she handed over two keys.

"I'm sure," she said, "I don't want 'em. I shall tell mother to return her keys, too, if that's the way you feel about it. Can't the pussies see the—"

"No," Cassie said.

"But I don't see why we can't run down and—"

"I prefer, Elsa," Leonidas said, "to allow Jock to display his surprise to me, himself."

"D'you mind," the little man said, "if I run down and look at the pickaxes?"

Cassie and Leonidas swallowed in unison.

"Pickaxes?" Leonidas said. "Er—what pickaxes?"

"Perfectly fine pickaxes," the little man said enthusiastically. "The colonel was telling me about them. Sounded like just what we need in the Water Department."

"You are—er—in the Water Department?" Leonidas inquired.

"Chief inspector," the judge said without much pride. "He's my husband. Really, Ernest, I don't think we have time to investigate pickaxes, now. I told you to have a man come out and demonstrate. Elsa, I hear the sleighs—"

Cassie drew a long breath of relief as the door closed at last behind the Rounds, Elsa, and the rest of her little charges.

"Bill, was that deliberate?"

"I don't think so," Leonidas said. "Are there—yes, there are sleighs at the corner. See? No, I think that to women like Elsa and the judge, there would be no mental obstacle in the way of using someone else's house for a waiting room. I don't think Elsa knew I was here."

"There were lights," Cassie said. "And the judge did. Oh, think of Dow letting himself get mixed up with Elsa, Bill! I can't imagine where his mind was at the time. Why, you can't even say she's got a nice figure. Or nice teeth. You can't even say well-of-course-she-has-brains. Oh, that girl does irritate me so. Rushing around, doing good all the time! Why, she even read to Medora when she had the grippe!"

Leonidas said he wondered if that were a wise step.

"I mean Medora," Cassie said. "Medora had the grippe. Not Elsa. Elsa never had a day's illness in her life. Didn't Estelle ever tell you? Not a day's sickness, and only one little silver filling in a molar. But of course, Elsa played up to Medora just hoping to heal the breach, and get Dow back in the will. Or get into it herself. So many people tried to worm their way into that will, after Medora and Dow fought. After all, she was rich, and she hadn't any other relations."

Leonidas looked at her speculatively.

"The love of money, as my old friend the Maharajah tritely says, is the root of all evil. M'yes. Cassie, where is Dow?"

"I can't think! I phoned Jock, and Dow left him at the Adamses' hours ago. Bill, d'you think we'd better stay here?"

"Why not?"

"Well," Cassie said, "I'm getting uneasy. There's simply no telling who will drop in next. Or what will happen. I feel harried."

"Which," Leonidas said, "is the way we are supposed to feel. Someone wishes that we would either tell about Medora, or else get thoroughly scared and clear out entirely. We're not going to do either."

"Bill, Jock's not being here isn't going to fool anyone about your surprise."

"Even small babes," Leonidas said, "seem to have figured that out. Even Elsa. M'yes. Come along, Cassie. I want to ask Cuff something."

"Oh, dear! Cuff is another problem. He's confused."

"About the body?"

"Oh, no," Cassie said. "I don't think he's given that a second thought. You know how he is. Sort of

Oriental about bodies. What's a body more or less—My, I wish I could feel that way! It's about Leslie. She confuses him."

"You never tried to tell her story to Cuff!"

"No. Oh, heavens, no! But Cuff got the impression that if you had a beautiful girl with luggage rushing around outside your house, dropping lipsticks in an intimate manner, she was your wife. Cuff is terribly moral about some things. Now he finds she isn't your wife, and he thinks you're both utterly abandoned. Explain to him very slowly that you're not. I do wish," she added, "that Margie would come back from her sister's. Cuff really needs her for an interpreter."

"M'yes," Leonidas said. "Cassie, how did that boy pass his police exams?"

"Wasn't it marvelous?" Cassie smiled brightly. "He was so pleased. He'd set his heart on being a cop, and he just worked so hard! When they get a thousand dollars saved up, he and Margie are going to get married. They'd have been all set last month, but Cuff took his bank-robber reward and put it on a horse named Marlene, in a weak moment. Now, explain to him about Leslie."

In words of one syllable, Leonidas explained to Cuff that Miss Horn was not his wife, but simply someone who happened to be passing by at the moment.

"There, see?" Cassie said. "Dow is going to marry her. D'you understand?"

"Where'd he meet her?" Cuff wanted to know.

"He hasn't, to the best of my knowledge," Leslie said. "Bill, here's your food. Look, can't we just say that I'm single, and Bill's single, and leave it at that? This matrimonial project you have in mind for me—"

"Oh, now you've got him looking reproachful again!" Cassie said. "Just as he was beginning to get it. Oh, well—Bill, what did you want to ask Cuff about?"

"This." Leonidas indicated the red refrigerator.

Cuff brightened. If people had to talk about things, he preferred things you could point at.

"That's a wow," he said with admiration that approached reverence. "That's a swell icebox, Bill. I'm going to get Margie an icebox like that. Only green. She likes green."

"Green is pretty," Leonidas said. "Now, Cuff, d'you know anything about the icebox racket?"

"You mean, a guy fixes up an old icebox, and paints it, and then talks somebody with a new icebox into thinking they got the wrong icebox, and then takes the new one and gives 'em the repaint. You mean like that?"

"Exactly," Leonidas said. "Do you know anything about it?"

"Sure, I used to work it with Slim O'Leary. I used to fix them up and carry 'em, and Slim did the chatter. Poor Slim! I tried to be a pal. I told him the colonel'd get him, and he better move on to Carnavon, but he wouldn't, and the colonel did. The colonel got him on the grass, too."

"What grass?"

"You know," Cuff said, "you see a guy's house needs a lawn, and you say you got sod, and does he wants some, and he says yes, and then you go to the nearest golf club and get some—"

"Cuff!" Cassie said. "Did you know the wretches who stole the seventh hole? You did! It cost the club three thousand to replace the turf, Bill. They were insured, of course, but Rutherford's on the Greens Committee, and he was simply fit to be tied."

"Yeah," Cuff said. "Poor Slim. That's why he got such a stretch. The colonel was plenty sore. But I got taken off that Daltondale beat, and up one place on the list."

"His first up," Cassie said brightly. "Isn't that marvelous? I told Rutherford that Cuff would be a help. He—er—do let me get you some more eggs, Bill. Don't you want some more eggs? They're fresh. I told my own egg man to come here. He has the brownest eggs in Dalton. I like brown eggs best, don't you? Do have some more!"

"Thank you, no," Leonidas said. "No more eggs." At some later date, he intended to discuss the origin and source of the inspiration for the removal of the seventh hole. Cuff never had thought that up by himself. "Cuff, who runs the icebox racket now that Slim is temporarily incommunicado?"

"Huh?"

"Who took on the icebox racket after Slim got put in jail? Who carries on?"

"Aw, nobody," Cuff said. "Not in this town. Not after what Slim got. And listen, Bill, you needn't never think nobody'd bother you, see? About that icebox, or nothing. Everybody knows you're a pal of mine, see? And the colonel's, too. Nobody wouldn't never try nothing on you. They wouldn't have the nerve, see?"

Cassie bestowed no more than a passing glance on the glass coffeepot that had slipped from her hands and shattered on the floor.

"Bill, aren't you smart! The icebox man wasn't a racket, was he? The brush man was real, because he sold you a whole set, like mine, and nothing happened while he was here. But the icebox man wasn't a racket at all—he was trying to get inside the house! Did he have one? Was it red?"

"If you mean, did he actually have a red refrigerator about his person," Leonidas said, "I don't know. I didn't see one. Nor do I remember either hearing or seeing any truck out front—"

"He just wanted to get in!" Cassie said. "That's what he wanted— Bill, what time did he come? When was he here?"

Leonidas answered her without any hesitation. He had been making mental timetables.

"He came first at ten-thirty. Then about eleven-fifteen, and the last time, around a quarter to twelve."

"Peters must have seen him, then," Cassie said. "If he came before noon, Peters must have seen him! Cuff, will Peters be in Car Fifteen now?"

Cuff glanced at the kitchen clock.

"Naw. He's off at five. But I can call him, if you want to find something out—"

"Wait," Leonidas said as Cuff reached for the red phone. "You've opened up a new train of thought, Cassie. Peters must be in a position to tell us a great deal, if he was in Car Fifteen from twelve until quarter past two. From his post on the corner, he could have seen—"

"No," Cassie shook her head. "I thought of Peters right away, Bill. But he won't be able to help us a single bit. You see, from noon till one-thirty, the cars have to go to the schools and look after the children, coming and going from their lunch. Rutherford simply boils about it, because he says it's just asking for noontime holdups, and the Retail Merchants say so, too. But the Safety Council wanted it, and got the Parent-Teachers Association to back them up, and there are more parents and teachers than merchants. And Rutherford can't say anything after those hideous pictures!"

"Aw, the one of me wasn't so worse," Cuff said. "Margie thought it was good only for around the mouth. She cut out the kid with a pair of shears I was holding the hand of, and put it in a frame."

"Er—the hand?" Leonidas asked.

"No, me. They had my name on it, too, Bill. It said, 'Officer Cornelius X. Murray guards Dalton kiddies from traffic—'" he paused.

"Hazards," Cassie said. "Or perils. Or something. Anyway, the parents and teachers thought it was fine that Dalton took such good care of the kiddies, so Rutherford can't say anything till there's a good noon holdup. Hm. I must remember about that."

"Say," Cuff said, "maybe we—"

"No!" Leonidas said. "You two do not engineer any noon holdups. Now, it is definitely a generally known fact that the prowl cars spend the midday interval in the vicinity of the schools?"

"Heavens, yes," Cassie said. "Mrs. Gibson next door to me practically has to go without lunch. Her Maggie used to refuse point-blank to get the children at noon, and now she drops everything and rushes off at eleven-thirty to get them. The school yards simply crawl with cooks and nursemaids. Some fine noon, of course, while the prowl-car men are leading kiddies across streets by the hand, something terrible will happen—Bill, that's what you're driving at, isn't it? Someone knew that Car Fifteen usually parked around the corner, so they just waited till they knew it wouldn't be there!"

Leonidas nodded.

"Personally," he said, "if I intended to commit a murder, I should try to pick a time when I knew for sure that the prowl car would be busy serving the kiddies. M'yes. I think I should get as much pleasure out of waiting till Colonel Carpenter's prowl car was gone as I'd get out of using Colonel Carpenter's pickax."

"Why, I've thought all along that someone was trying to make a fool out of Rutherford!" Cassie said. "But I can't think who. People like Rutherford. He hasn't any enemies, has he, Cuff?"

"Show 'em to me," Cuff said simply.

"Rossi, perhaps?" Leonidas said.

"Aw, no, Rossi likes the colonel," Cuff said. "He's getting up a fund to give the colonel a watch on his birthday. You're all wrong about Rossi, Mrs. Price. Maybe he's taken a little cut once in a while, but he

likes the colonel. I never once heard Rossi say nothing about the colonel that it wasn't something good.
He thinks the colonel is a fine man."

Leonidas twirled his pince-nez.

"What about Medora?" he asked.

"No," Cassie said positively. "When Medora got
mad at anyone, she told them so. Only last week, she
gave Rutherford some money for the new pistol range
he wants and the city won't spend the money for.
I'll give Medora credit. When she was annoyed about
something or at someone, she came right out in the
open and said so. Just the way she threatened you."

"Aunt Medora threatened Bill?" Leslie asked in
amazement.

"Yes. She was furious about this house. She didn't
like it. She said she'd run Bill out of town," Cassie
said, "and because Dow was the architect, and her
nephew, she got mad at Dow and disinherited him.
Didn't I explain all about that part, dear?"

"You missed that," Leslie rumpled her curls with
a quick gesture. "You—er—you skipped around some,
you know."

Leonidas bit his lip and tried not to smile. He
could imagine how Cassie might have summed things
up for Leslie's benefit during that interval while he
had entertained the Pussycats in the living room. As

a matter of fact, he admired the girl for maintaining her composure. A lesser spirit might well have gone a little berserk.

"Well, dear," Cassie said, "Dow's the one who wants to marry you—Lord knows where he is. He ought to be here. Bill, it simply amazes me, the amount we've found out without even leaving this house. Someone came here between twelve and two-fifteen, and Medora came with them—she must have, mustn't she?"

"If you mean that Medora Winthrop must have been alive when she came here, yes," Leonidas said. "Otherwise, I think we could reasonably assume that the place would have been a shambles."

"And they knew the police car wouldn't be here. I don't like that." Cassie said. "That smacks of a lot of planning. I don't like that part."

"I don't either," Leslie said. "What with me walking around in a starving condition most of that time. No one is ever going to believe that. In fact, I don't think anyone's going to believe any part of my story. I don't know that I blame them. The only thing that soothes me to any extent is that I have no motive for killing Medora Winthrop. And I know absolutely nothing about the habits of Dalton police cars. Or about Dalton, either. Look, I'm awfully confused about this icebox man."

"Me, too," Cuff said. "Look, Bill, you mean a guy come here about a icebox? Was that what you wanted to ask Peters about?"

"That's right," Leonidas said encouragingly. Any trace of such tremendous mental percolating on the part of Cuff was something, he thought, that ought to be encouraged. "That's it. Now, you call Peters and ask him if he saw a man wandering around here—"

"Listen, Bill, what did the guy look like?"

"He was a nondescript individual," Leonidas said, "who might have been peddling shoestrings. His only characteristic appeared to be persistency."

"Yeah," Cuff said. "Uh-huh. Was he short, like? And sort of dark? And he had on like a Mackinaw, with a zipper? And pig eyes?"

"Cuff," Leonidas said with admiration, "that is as masterly a description as I have ever heard. Brief. Concise. Pointed. You have undoubtedly known this man over a period of years!"

Cuff shook his head.

"I don't know him, Bill!"

"But you must!" Leonidas said. "You—"

"Let me, Bill," Cassie said. "That isn't the right way. Look, Cuff, when did you see Pig Eyes? Was it this morning?"

"Yeah," Cuff said. "I'm coming out of the dispensary, see, and the doctor says the wrist'll be all right day after tomorrow. And there's a truck stuck in a snow drift on the corner, and there's a red icebox in it, see?"

"Like Bill's," Cassie said.

"Yeah, that's right. I thinks, there's an icebox like Bill's. And the guy says will I give him a hand, and I shows him my wrist, see? But I get in the truck, see, and cut it for him while he digs and puts on ashes. And we get it out. So when I go, I tell him that's a snappy job he's got on, and he says it's a special job he just got from the warehouse. That wasn't no repaint, Bill. That was a new box. Brand new."

"Cuff, that's marvelous!" Cassie said. "Now we can phone the distributor, or the warehouse, and find out who—"

Leonidas interrupted her.

"Don't let's lose the thread. Cuff, Pig Eyes was alone, he had a truck, and on the truck was a red refrigerator like mine, and Pig Eyes told you it was a special job. Did he tell you anything else, as where the box was going, or what he was doing with it?"

Cuff shook his head.

"He didn't say nothing. But he asked me if Main Avenue'd be cleared so he could go up it."

"Which means," Cassie was getting excited, "that he was coming up here to Birch Hill. Now, all we've got to do is to phone and find out who ordered it, and then we'll know who wanted to get in. And then we'll know who killed Medora. Why, it's marvelous!" She paused and looked at Leonidas. "Oh. Isn't it?"

"In the first place," he pointed out, "it's too late to call warehouses or distributors, Cassie. And I greatly doubt if the name given by the purchaser will do us any good."

Cassie wanted to know why.

"If," Leonidas said, "I found myself compelled for some obscure reason to whisk your icebox away and replace it with another new icebox, and if I wished the whole affair to be shrouded with deep secrecy, I should order the new one in your name, pay cash, and cause my own hireling to make delivery in his truck. But my name would never be involved in the purchase, and my hireling would be deliberately chosen for his inability, if questioned, to remember who I was. M'yes. Now, why didn't I notice any truck, I wonder?"

"Probably he pulled it around on the back street," Cuff said. "It ain't so far to your back door from there. That's where your driveway is, anyhow. You can't tell, because it ain't cleared out. But the drive like for an icebox would be to the back."

"He means," Cassie translated, "the service drive is

at the rear. What a lot someone knows, Bill! About prowl cars, and your refrigerator being red, and the service drive at the rear— Let's call Peters and see if he can cast any light."

But Peters, as he assured both Cassie and Cuff in the course of a lengthy telephone conversation, remembered seeing no trucks in general, and no specific truck with an icebox on it.

Cassie sighed as she hung up.

"The first whiff of a real clew, and we can't get anywhere with it! Cuff, don't you remember the truck's number? Wasn't there a name on the side, like Joe's Express, or something?"

Cuff said plaintively that he wasn't on duty.

"Besides," he added, "the plates was all covered with snow."

Leonidas smiled.

"Were they, indeed. All covered with snow. And although Pig Eyes was willing to chat with you, he didn't allow his truck to be seen by Peters. He drove around the far block and avoided that particular corner where Car Fifteen was. Cuff, if you could whip your brain into recalling more of Pig Eyes and his truck, I should present you and Margie with a green refrigerator for your wedding present."

Cuff rubbed his nose and stared into the corner.

"Bill," he said, "I never thought harder than I'm

thinking now. You look in it while I keep on thinking."

"In what?"

"In the box. If he wants it, there's something in it, see?"

Cassie let out a war whoop.

"Of course! No one's going to invest in a new de luxe Frosty Spot just for the fun of it! What did you say, Bill?"

"It was an aside," Leonidas was busy removing the contents of the red refrigerator, "concerning babes and sucklings. You take the lower shelves—"

Two minutes later, they surveyed the assortment of provisions strewn over the kitchen.

"Unless someone's hidden something in an egg," Leslie said, "I think we're wrong. What about the works?"

"They're all sealed," Cassie said. "That's one of the reasons we chose it. The works are all sealed up, and once every hundred years you have a man open them with a blowtorch and put in a new works. Cuff, you see if there's anything in the works."

"Sure," Cuff said. "Got a screw driver?"

Leonidas felt a twinge of pain as Cuff deftly proceeded to reduce his beautiful streamlined icebox to an unsightly, utilitarian hulk.

Then, with the same deftness, he put it all together again.

"I bow to you," Leonidas said sincerely. "I should still be struggling with the first little screw head."

"Gee, Bill, I guess I was wrong. There ain't nothing in the works or the motor or the unit or the insulation. Nobody ain't touched nothing, neither. I can tell. But if there ain't something somebody wants, what does somebody want it for? I sort of think that's kind of queer— Say, Bill, I think I just heard someone at the front door. Like a key."

"Bison," Leonidas said with resignation. "Don't you think Bison, Cassie?"

"Bison?"

"I've no doubt," Leonidas said, "that all the Bison in Dalton wear my door key on their watch chains, along with ornamental teeth, and claws. Oh."

Dow lounged against the doorway. He was hatless and disheveled, and his face was blotched with cold.

"Dow!" Cassie said. "Where have you— For heaven's sakes, Dow!"

"Go on, laugh," Dow said wearily. "I know I'm a mess. I— Where did you find *her*? Where did she come from?"

"She dropped in," Cassie said. "Her name is Leslie Horn. She isn't married."

Dow walked across the kitchen and gravely kissed Cassie's cheek.

"I *knew* you'd be delighted," Cassie said. "And she knows you want to marry her. I told her so."

"You were the one on the train!" Leslie said.

"Didn't I tell you that, dear?" Cassie said. "He had to fuss around with Bill instead of doing anything about you, and it simply gnawed at his vitals. You were just a fox—"

"Cassie," Dow said, "I don't feel that you're advancing my case. I never said she was a fox. I said she was the most beautiful thing I ever saw, and I intended to marry the lovely creature, and I do, but I haven't the time for any courting right now. Listen—"

"You listen to us, first!" Cassie said. "We have—"

"Both of you," Leonidas said, "be still. Dow, this is, in substance, what has taken place here since you left. Listen carefully, and if Cassie shows any signs of saying a word, gag her."

His summing up took him just four minutes by the clock.

As he listened, Dow's worried look gave way to a grin. By the time Leonidas concluded, he was shaking with laughter.

"After hearing that, Bill, nothing matters," he said. "I was worried when I came here, but now all I can think of is the Maharajah—what was that? About the snake and the thunderstorm?"

" 'He who is in the grasp of the cobra,' " Leonidas said, " 'can smile at the lightning's forked tongue.' M'yes. I like that. I think it has a certain ring. Er— what's been happening to you?"

"I can't sum it up the way you did— Say, Leslie, did you see Elsa? Oh, what a pity! Elsa and the Pussycats. Tudbury's Horse! Wow! Well, I took Jock to the Adamses', and as I cut back to Main Avenue, I went past our house, and there was mother stuck in a snow drift."

"In all my life," Leonidas said reflectively, "I have never before heard of so many people being stuck in so many snow drifts."

Dow pointed out that there were a lot of snow drifts.

"And mother had practically buried her car in one. You see, she feels if you race an engine hard enough, anything's possible, and she was simply incredulous when I told her that her rear end'd fallen out. She said she didn't believe it, but if it had, I was to drive her into Boston at once. When I declined, there were bitter words," Dow added, "about filial gratitude. Following which, I presented her with my car, and told her to go along. So she did. And before she even got to the corner, she slewed into the Parrs' driveway post, and lost one chain. And I considered the situation, and decided that while I could get back here in a cab, we really needed a vehicle on tap. So I summoned the tow car from the garage, and on the way back to the garage with it and mother's car, I hopped off at Paddock Street—"

"And went to my house," Cassie said. "And took Popeye from my drive—didn't I leave Popeye in the drive?"

"Yes, dear," Dow said. "You left Popeye in the drive, with the keys in it, but Popeye was frozen, so I pushed it back into the garage and took the sedan. Cassie, whatever inspired you to buy that black sedan?"

"Rutherford," Cassie said. "He said Popeye wasn't dignified for his sister to drive around in what amounted to a soapbox on wheels, so I got Simeon. It was the most dignified car I could find. It needs gas—"

"Yes. I know. I noticed. So I drove up to the village to get some. And just as the fellow started the gas pump, an Upper Falls bus stopped at the corner for the lights. I didn't think anything of it, at first, but my eyes kept sort of straying to it, and then, just as it started off, I realized— Are you listening? I realized that Swiss Chard was on it!"

Cassie squealed.

"Chard? What was she on an Upper Falls bus for?"

"That," Dow said, "is something we will probably never know."

"What was she doing?"

"Just sitting on the bus, being transported. I had to wait for the gas, and pay the man, and then I followed the bus. That wasn't hard, because those busses are pretty lumbering, anyway, and with the snow, it wasn't making very rapid headway. So I followed it."

"M'yes," Leonidas said. "Did it occur to you that—"

"That I might dash ahead of the bus, and leave Cassie's car, and hop on the bus myself? Oh, yes," Dow said. "I thought of that one. But I couldn't get past the thing. The street was only cleared for two lanes, and what with the streetcars and the west-bound traffic, I never got the chance. I tried. God knows I tried. I did everything but hurdle that damn bus— That reminds me, Cassie. Have the bill for the fender and the new radiator grille sent me. That's what I got for trying."

"They don't cost much," Cassie said consolingly. "The man gives me the grilles wholesale, you know. What a pity you didn't have Popeye!"

"Or even my own car," Dow said. "I could have got by with either. But you could put my car and

Popeye in that damn black sedan and still have room
for two tables of bridge. Anyway, I consoled myself
by thinking that maybe it would be better if I waited
and saw what she did. She got off at Lake and Water—"

"Oh, dear!" Cassie said. "I know what happened
there. There wasn't any place to park. Was there?
There never is!"

"Is that that place," Leonidas said, "where the
streetcar line stops in a square?"

Dow nodded.

"It's also the junction of Routes Seven, Eighteen,
and One-thirty-four-A, and several others I don't remember. Finally I drove Simeon into a snow bank
and started out on foot along Water Street after her.
She turned— Cuff, is there anything the matter with
you that you make those peculiar sounds?"

"I'm thinking," Cuff said.

"Oh. Well, I followed Chard at what I thought
was a discreet distance, but after a while she started
to turn back and take little peeks at me. Then she
walked faster. So I walked a little faster. At a brisk
trot," Dow said wearily, "we traversed practically all
of Dalton Upper Falls. Finally I stopped in a doorway on Florence Street—you know that section, Bill?
It's just beginning to degenerate from frame houses
with cupolas into three-family tenements. And Chard
paused, and looked around, and then she started off

like mad, in a terrific rush. So I rushed. And she turned back to Water Street. And before I realized, that wench opened her mouth and started to scream 'Stop Thief,' and point at me. What does Rutherford feed his cops for breakfast?"

"I gather," Leonidas said, "that Dalton's finest were on the job?"

"On the job, and apparently on their marks, just waiting for someone to yell 'Stop Thief.' One weighed about two-fifty and had the speed of an antelope—"

"Mac Ardle," Cuff said. "He's an old marathoner."

"I don't doubt it. The other was lighter, with a pointed face, and he ran like two antelopes."

"Pimcek," Cuff said. "He used to be anchor on the Golden Rule Athaletic Club relay. Say, you mean them two chased you, and you got away?"

"In my day," Dow said, "people have pinned medals on my chest for the way I ran. Hear that, Leslie? Advt. But I never ran for dear old Dumbert or the dear old college the way I ran from those two cops. I wasn't going to have Swiss Chard get me for being a bag-snatcher. So I circled back to the car."

"I know," Cassie said. "And then they got you for parking Simeon near a hydrant. That's what always happens to me on Water Street."

"No, darling," Dow said. "No. Swiss Chard was pointing at the car, and telling two more of Rutherford's finest that the young cur who tried to snatch her bag had followed her on the bus in that selfsame car. I couldn't hear what she said, but it was obvious to a child from the way she gestured up the street, and at the car, and then at her bag."

"Whereupon," Leslie said unexpectedly, "whereupon the gallant young officer seized Disguise Kit Number Six from his pocket, and in a trice had transformed himself into the very counterpart of Ivan, the sneering young aide of Prince Casimir Vassily."

Dow threw back his head and howled with laughter.

"Ah, the incomparable Lieutenant Haseltine! There, there's a common bond. I could never marry a woman who didn't love Prince Casimir of the sinister mustache and the nitroglycerin. But d'you know, the funniest part is that's who I *did* think of! Haseltine. So I ducked into an alley, and turned my trench coat inside out, and stuck on a beret I had in my pocket, and put on my driving glasses. And then I strolled past the car in time to hear Rutherford's finest promise Swiss Chard that they'd stay right there till the guy came back to his car. They looked as if they meant it, so I took the next Upper Falls bus back to the village, and then the Birch Hill bus over here. Filling Simeon's gas tank was a capital outlay. I couldn't afford a cab."

"Did Miss Chard recognize you? Did she know

who you were?" Leonidas asked. "And why didn't you follow her, Dow, and see where she went?"

"I couldn't tell whether she recognized me or not," Dow said. "You can't tell anything from that frightened manner of hers. You can't tell what she thinks from the way she looks. But she had the cops so upset with her fright that one of 'em said he'd take her wherever she was going and make sure she wasn't bothered again."

"Listen, Bill," Cuff said plaintively, "who was it got bumped off here, anyway?"

"Medora Winthrop. Miss Medora Winthrop," Leonidas said. "I'm sorry nobody thought to tell you. D'you know her?"

"I think I had a car of hers once," Cuff said casually. "Look, who's this Prince Somebody?"

"Is there anyone here," Dow said, "who feels competent to explain Prince Casimir Vassily to Cuff?"

"Now, Dow," Cassie said, "don't confuse him! Cuff, that's just someone in a book. Like—well, like Tarzan. You know. In a book. Have you got it straight? The woman who was killed was Miss Medora Winthrop. The prince is just somebody in a book. If you could—if you liked to read better, I'd let you take one of the books home. You'd adore Lieutenant Haseltine."

"That reminds me," Dow said, "I've forgotten to

give you Jock's parting message. He said to tell Bill to remember Cannae. You happen to know about Haseltine and Cannae, Bill?" He gave Leonidas no chance to answer. "After about two hundred and twenty-five pages of pure and unadulterated buffeting by every fate known to man, Haseltine thinks of Cannae."

"M'yes," Leonidas said. "M'yes, indeed. Cannae. That historic battle between the Romans and the Carthaginians, fought in Apulia in the year 216 B. C., in which the small, weak army of Hannibal cut the incomparable forces of eighty-five thousand proud Roman legionaries to pieces—"

"To shreds," Leslie said.

"To shreds. In that," Leonidas continued, "by means of an ingenious strategical concentration, it caught the enemy from the flank with cavalry, and surrounded him. Clausewitz and Schlieffen, of the Prussian General Staff, elaborated the idea of Cannae into a general theoretical doctrine, and then compressed the doctrine into an exact strategical system. That, in brief, is Cannae."

"Well, you've certainly read Haseltine!" Dow said. "Somehow, I didn't expect that of a Meredith man. Well, Jock said I was to remind you."

Leonidas nodded slowly.

"And definitely," he said, "I think it's time that

Cannae was recalled to me. M'yes. Definitely. Cassie, phone headquarters and say that your car has been stolen, you don't know when, but it's gone, and will someone be good enough to find it and return it to you here. That will take care of that. Cuff—"

"Yeah, Bill, we better get going," Cuff said. "We better go after her right away."

Leonidas surveyed Cuff thoughtfully through his pince-nez.

His own plans had not been entirely formulated, although the general line of indicated action was clear in his mind.

First of all, a vehicle was required, so Cassie's car must be returned. He knew that it would be, without hesitation or question, once the police learned that it was hers. The Dalton police, on the whole, were Cassie's willing if somewhat puzzled slaves. They enjoyed doing things for the colonel's sister, and they had done much funnier things than return a supposedly stolen car to her.

After the car was returned, Leonidas intended to seek out the officer who had accompanied Miss Chard from Water Street, and from him discover where Miss Chard had gone. Cassie could wangle that.

Most important of all, Miss Chard had to be found. If she had remained in Dalton this long, the chances appeared excellent that she would continue to remain in Dalton. It was imperative, at this point, that she be found and compelled to answer several vital questions.

And Leonidas intended that she should.

But he had not expected Cuff's mind to react along similar lines. Cuff had only just become aware of the identity of the murdered woman. It did not seem remotely possible that he could have grasped the part Miss Chard played, or assimilated the necessity for finding her. Certainly, Cuff wouldn't know where Miss Chard was.

"Er—where?" Leonidas asked. "Where do you suggest we go, Cuff?"

"Halfway up Arthur," Cuff struggled into his yellow polo coat. "That's where she is. Let's get going."

CHAPTER VII

"CUFF," Cassie said severely, "you're letting your-self get carried away! Whoever Arthur is, I'm sure Miss Chard—really, that's practically indecent. Arthur who?"

"Arthur Street," Cuff said.

"One of the Daltonville Streets?" Cassie said. "Why, I never knew Miss Chard even knew any of the Daltonville Streets!"

"Not Daltonville. Upper Falls," Cuff said.

Cassie clucked her tongue.

"Halfway up Arthur! I never heard of such a thing!"

"You don't know them streets like I do," Cuff returned. "Look, Mrs. Price. Here's Florence Street. See?" he drew a line in the air with his finger. "You go down Water Street off Upper Falls Square, like this, and here's Florence. And off Florence is Kitty's Alley, like this. And then next there's Arthur Street, see? Arthur's off Florence, right about here. And half-way up Arthur is here. And that's where she is."

"I'm glad, cousin," Dow said, "to note a faint flush

in your cheeks. I hope you're squelched. Go on, Cuff.
Arthur's off Florence, and Florence is where Chard
and I played tag."

Cuff nodded.

"Yeah. I been thinking and thinking, see, and when
you said Florence, something begun to click. Halfway
up Arthur is the garage. Only it's more of an old
livery stable, like. And that's the place I been trying
to think of, all along."

"You mean, Miss Chard is in a stable, like?" Cassie
demanded.

Cuff looked at her wonderingly.

"Who?"

"Oh, dear!" Cassie said. "Oh, dear me! Cuff, what
about the stable? Who is in the stable? I'm beginning
to think you're out of your mind! What about your
old stable halfway up Arthur? You said she was there.
Who?"

"See, Mrs. Price," Cuff said patiently, "that's where
he keeps her—"

"Who, Miss Chard? Who keeps Miss Chard in a
stable?" Cassie said. "It's absurd. I don't believe it. I
don't believe Miss Chard was ever kept in a stable
by anyone, ever. I don't think she ever set foot in a
stable!"

Cuff sighed.

"See, Mrs. Price. See here. You get it about Arthur,

don't you? And on Arthur, halfway up, there's this garage, like. And there's where he keeps her. The truck—look, Bill, you get it, don't you?"

"I think," Leonidas said, "that I begin to. M'yes. Of course. Halfway up Arthur Street in Dalton Upper Falls is a former livery stable now used as a garage, and that is where Pig Eyes keeps his truck."

"Yeah, sure!" Cuff said. "That's it. And we should ought to get going and see about her. On account Pig Eyes might take her—"

"Her!" Cassie said with deep scorn. "Her! Whoever heard of anyone referring to a truck as *her!*"

Cuff scratched the side of his nose.

"Well, gee," he said, "I always do. I don't think I never heard nobody call a truck *him.* Only her. Like somebody says where's your car, and you say you'll get her. Like boats. *Her.*"

"I'll concede boats," Cassie said, "but I don't see how you could possibly think of a great lumbering beast of a throbbing truck as *her!*"

"The point," Leonidas said, "is, after all, not the gender of a truck, Cassie. The point is that the truck belonging to Pig Eyes is to be found in the Arthur Street garage—"

"I know," Cassie said. "I know. I'm just carping because I resent having been so stupid. Bill, that's what she was on Florence Street, and in that vicinity for, wasn't it? She was going to find Pig Eyes. She was the one who hired him! Cuff, I think you're marvelous!"

"Aw," Cuff said, "it wasn't nothing. I knew if I thought long enough, I'd think where I seen that truck once before. There wasn't no name on it, but I seen it somewheres, and I only just had to think where. Say, Mrs. Price, you better call about your car now," he paused with his hand on the back-door knob, "and I'll go tell the boys in Car Fifteen they should park out front, huh?"

"Why?" Leonidas asked. "Cassie, phone!"

"Why, so as nobody won't come inside here while we're all gone out. But what'll I tell 'em?"

"Tell 'em," Cassie picked up the red phone, "that Mr. Witherall lost his other key ring, the one with his— Police headquarters, please. The one with his name and address on the tag. Wait. Police headquarters? This is Mrs. Price. Oh, hello, Anderson. How are Lucille's tonsils? Oh, I'm awfully glad. That's fine! Anderson, someone's stolen my black sedan! Yes! I just looked out—"

After a lengthy conversation, during the course of which Cassie explained in detail about her stolen sedan, and offered many helpful hints on tonsillectomies and their aftercare, Cassie finally set down the receiver.

"He says he thinks they already know where it is, and he'll have it sent right up. With his name and address on the tag, Cuff. And—"

Leonidas interrupted her.

"But is it worth the effort, I wonder? Cuff, should you honestly be deterred from your purpose of wilfully entering my house, merely by the presence of Car Fifteen? That is to say," he realized that Cuff was getting confused again, "if you wished to get into this house, would a prowl car parked out front disturb you in the least?"

"Gee, I don't think so," Cuff said after a moment's reflection. "I'd put in a fake call to the other side of the hill here, see? And then get in while they was gone to answer it."

"Exactly," Leonidas said. "So, why bother with Car Fifteen? On the other—"

"But we must be able to lock the doors!" Cassie said. "There must be some way we can fix things, Dow! Isn't there?"

Dow shook his head.

"I made two errors in this house," he said. "I did too good a job in segregating the garage and the maid's room. Everybody who saw this house had that excellent segregation pointed out. Everyone knew that the back door and this part of the house were as another world. I took pleasure in explaining to people how Mr. Witherall would never be disturbed. If I hadn't tried so hard for seclusion, this never could have happened. And I *ought* to have installed electric eyes, Bill. I thought of 'em. But short of a complete door and window electric eye or electric lock installation, I don't think anything can help us now. Bill's right, Cassie. If someone set his heart on getting in here, police cars wouldn't stop him. Nothing would."

"Pooh!" Cassie said. "A door barricade would discourage me!"

"For how long?" Dow asked. "Just about two seconds. Then you'd hop up on a snow bank, and shinny up to the sun deck, and pick a window lock. Someone'll have to stay here— Cuff, if you knew that someone was in a house, would you break and enter just the same?"

Cuff said it would all depend.

"Me, I wouldn't. If there's one person, you can't never tell there ain't two, so you'd need a rod, and then you get away from things like just breaking and entering in the night, into—"

"Armed robbery," Cassie said, "and assault and battery with dangerous weapons, and mayhem, and all. Bill, I know how we can settle it. Leslie and Dow can both stay here."

Leslie and Dow both protested vehemently.

"D'you think," Leslie said, "after all I've gone

through, I'm going to sit here quietly with—well, with a milk bottle in my hand, or a bread knife, or something, scaring away Tudbury's Horse, while you go gallivanting off, finding that Chard woman? Not much! I've got a few pungent words to say to Chard, myself! I'm going!"

"So'm I," Dow said. "After the way she foxed me, I'm going to have the last tag. Stay here? Not, as my esteemed mother says, not on your tintype! No, sir!"

"Both of you are going to sit right here," Cassie said. "You can barricade the front door, and fix things so no one can get down the stairs from the second floor without your knowing it, and—"

"And have a nice game of casino here in the kitchen!" Dow said. "Or maybe Russian bank."

"Dear me," Cassie looked at him, "aren't you stupid? Aren't you a great goon! You spent the entire morning and forenoon discussing her eyes and her teeth and her hair and her lovely voice, and now you—"

"Suppose," Leslie said quickly, "that Tudbury's Horse came trooping back? How could we stop them any more than you could? Suppose those little girls drop in again to wait for their bus home? We can hardly lay violent hands on a lot of little innocent children!"

"On second thought," Dow said, "Cassie has the right idea. This is the best place for us, Leslie. We can sit here by the back door and read Haseltine aloud, the picture of perfect domesticity. Haven't you got some Haseltine, Bill?"

"That's a beautiful picture!" Leslie said. "Tudbury's Horse knows me as a nurse. What would happen if they burst in while you were reading to me about Prince Casimir and Irma?"

"I should unhesitatingly introduce you as my wife," Dow said promptly. "Estelle Otis will faint, and Tudbury's Horse will exit en masse, bearing her limp body away."

"There, see?" Cassie said to Leonidas. "I said that all he needed was a little push. This day has just done him a world of good. Leslie, I know that you and Dow can cope with anything. Just you think of Lieutenant Haseltine, and do what he'd do. Anyway, Tudbury's Horse won't be back. You needn't give them a second thought. They'll all be at that meeting of the Women Voters and Taxpayers League, down at the auditorium."

"That place again?" Leslie said. "Don't the women of Dalton do anything else but sit in an auditorium? Do they spend all their time there?"

"It's one of those days," Cassie said, "when the Tuesday Club lecture-luncheon just happens to fall on the same day as the monthly meeting of the League. It's a tremendous meeting tonight, with door prizes and the Legion band. I'm supposed to be there, sitting on the platform in my black lace."

Dow chuckled.

"So was mother, I think. She wouldn't admit it on a bed of thorns, but she loathes that League— Cass, how come you ever got mixed up with that outfit?"

"I started it, dear," Cassie said with a little sigh. "But that was a long time ago. Years and years ago, but it wasn't the same thing at all, then. We were suffragettes."

"Cassie," Leonidas said, "were you a suffragette?"

Cassie beamed.

"Oh, my, yes! Didn't you know? Why, I can't tell you *how* many times I was arrested! Practically every day. Anyway, I started the League, way back there. But after we got the vote, it petered out, and it bored me, so I never went. Then about six years ago, it came to life again, being militant about taxes— Didn't your mother have a hand in that, Dow?"

"You know mother," Dow said. "She never let a chance to be militant about taxes get by her, if she saw it first. But now it's different, isn't it?"

"Completely," Cassie said. "They went through a sort of intermediate state, after the tax fusses. You know, they passed a lot of resolutions condemning Hitler and Mussolini, and they sent a lot of encouraging telegrams to Haile Selassie and Schussnigg. But

now— Cuff, will you look out the front door and see
if there's any sign of the car? But now, they're all
mixed up with local politics. Clean Government for
Dalton, and who's the best alderman from Ward
Four—"

"Clambakes," Cuff said as he crossed the kitchen.
"That's the Voters League, ain't it? They give clambakes, and free milk. There's some talk they're going
to put up Scipione for mayor."

"Who?" Cassie said.

"Mike Scipione. He's a Ward Four man. Whoever
they put up, they'll elect him, after them clambakes
and the free milk, and the free ice cream, and Beano,
and all. Margie won a seventeen-jewel solid gold watch
to the Beano one night."

"It was the Beano angle that alienated mother,"
Dow said. "Beano and Ward Four. Mother's for free
milk, but she didn't like the," he looked at Cuff's
derby, "the headgear and the cigar smoke. Well, if
the League's got Ward Four lined up, I guess our re-
form administration's on the way out. Rutherford'll
be out, too— What did you say, Bill?"

"Should you say," the pince-nez were twirling,
Cassie noticed, "should you say, offhand, that the
mayorship of Dalton—er—led to higher things?"

Dow nodded.

"As a rule, it's considered a step in the right direction. It's worth a term in Congress, if anyone wants the job, and sometimes they get shoved into the lieutenant-governorship. I think a couple got to be governors— Bill, do you think there's a hookup between Chard and this refrigerator lad?"

"Of course there is," Cassie said. "There must be. I just can't get over Swiss Chard's knowing her way about Florence Street, and that section—of course, she was going to that garage to see Pig Eyes. And even if neither happens to be there now, we can find out where they went. Is that the car now, Cuff? I'll go thank Anderson—"

She bustled out of the kitchen.

Dow turned to Leonidas.

"Bill, what do you really think? About Chard, I mean?"

"What I think," Leonidas said, "would amaze you. It is amazing me. Dow, people may come here whom you cannot keep out—"

"You mean, Rutherford, perhaps?"

"Possibly. But I depend on you to keep people away from downstairs. I don't think for one moment that we're ever going to fool the colonel, but everyone else must be made to feel that we have never been in that garage, and that we will never enter it till Jock comes."

"We'll brazen it out," Dow said. "I'll promise you

that anyone who enters that garage will have to step over my dead body. What's the idea behind things, Bill? Do people want the body found?"

"I think they did, at first. Now they realize we're not going to bring the matter up, so they wish we would depart. For what purpose," Leonidas added, "I do not know. Dow, did Miss Chard have any relatives?"

Dow looked surprised.

"Why, I suppose she must have, mustn't she? I never thought of her having any family, any more than I thought of her having a first name. After all, Bill, she wasn't the sort who led you into a corner and told you about her uncle who drank."

"She has a brother," Leslie said. "She mentioned him to me this morning. His name is George, and he's a musician, and she'd have told me his life story if I'd given her a chance. She was all wound up about George."

"Well," Dow said, "that was your influence. I hadn't seen you more than half a second on the train this morning before I wanted to tell you about my life insurance, and how much I made, and if you'd share my pottage—"

"We've had enough," Leslie said firmly, "of all that!"

"I like that firm touch," Dow said. "Look, you like

this house, don't you? Well, I'll build you one like it. With a nice studio and lovely north light, and you can paint your head off. And—"

"Where did Medora keep objects of value?" Leonidas asked.

"In the Dalton National's largest safety deposit box," Dow said. "I used to beg to go to the vault with her, when I was a kid, so I could crawl in the vacant space when the box was taken out. She had a smaller box for the family jewels, and a still smaller one for petty cash. She was a pushover for petty cash on hand."

"You mean," Leonidas said, "that she—er—hoarded dimes? Or possibly nickels?"

"Just bills," Dow said. "I don't think anything ever gave her any greater pleasure than Roosevelt's bank holiday. She'd always said that her petty cash would be needed some day, and a time would come, and it did. She financed half Dalton for a few days."

"Did she ever keep valuables in her house?" Leonidas said. "Up here, on the hill?"

Dow looked at him wonderingly.

"You do ask," he said, "the oddest things, Bill! I don't know whether she did or not. There was a little safe in the library. One of those iron boxes with a wreath of roses painted on the door. Cuff could probably open it with a thumbtack, or his thumbnail. It said 'Chauncey Winthrop Dow' on it. By the way, Leslie, my name is Chauncey Winthrop Dow. You'll have to be told, sooner or later."

"Good," Leslie said. "That settles it. I never could look with any degree of seriousness on a man named Chauncey. It reminds me of a buttered ear of corn. There! That whole business is now settled."

"Who," Leonidas said quickly before Dow could answer, "who was Medora's heir, ultimately?"

Dow shrugged.

"For all I know, she endowed a home for trained mice, or old circus horses. She may have left everything to Elsa. Or she may have— Bill, suppose she left it to Swiss Chard! I never thought of that!"

"D'you think that's at all likely?" Leonidas asked.

"Medora liked her," Dow said, "or she'd have fired her. And Chard must have liked Medora, or she'd have left, years ago. In our last interview, Aunt Medora touched at length on the topic of ungrateful relatives, and how none of hers would ever touch a penny of her money— Bill, that must be the answer. Medora made a will in favor of Chard. She must have! She— Are you all set, Cassie?"

"Yes," Cassie bustled back into the kitchen. "Anderson brought the car himself, because he wanted to ask me about a gargle for Lucille— Bill, aren't you ready? What *have* you been doing? And where are your overshoes? You must put your overshoes on!"

"George didn't," Leslie said.

"Come, come!" Cassie clucked her tongue. "Really, dear, we've had enough of that sort of thing, don't you think? Halfway up Arthur and now George didn't —George didn't what?"

"George didn't put his overshoes on," Leslie said. "Chard's brother George. He didn't put his overshoes on."

"Why, dear?"

"I don't know," Leslie said. "But that's what she told me. Brother George, she said very distinctly, did *not* put on his overshoes. That's one of the tidbits about brother George that she told me before I turned the subject into other channels. She seemed pretty upset about George not wearing his galoshes. She told me at least twice."

"I always say," Cassie remarked, "you can't tell a thing about mousy women. Why, I never knew she had a brother George! And what a quaint thing to tell you about him, too! Bill, isn't it strange that Swiss Chard should pause and discuss her brother's overshoes with what amounted to a perfect stranger? I should have thought she'd have been too terrified."

"That's the way I feel," Dow said. "Like that plane. Bill said she went for Leslie in a plane, and had another waiting to bring Leslie back to Dalton, but the snowstorm interfered. Now I can't see Chard getting into a plane at the point of a gun. Not even if Aunt Medora stood behind the gun. I can't swallow that picture of Chard whisking around in planes. Of course, I suppose there's a certain efficiency about Chard—"

"She was marvelous with accounts," Cassie said. "Medora always said that. And ordering."

"Oh, she probably could pinch a melon with the best," Dow said. "But I still can't see what goaded her into whisking around so, and biffing people left and right. I'll grant her strength of character, but I think something must have been goading her, don't you, Bill?"

Leonidas nodded. He had come to that decision some hours before.

"Where is my luggage, Cassie?" he asked.

"At my house—oh, I completely forgot," Cassie said. "Dow and that limousine chauffeur dumped it at my house this morning. Are your overshoes in it somewhere? They are? Well, you'll have to take Dow's. Get them for him, Dow, while I fetch your heavy coat from the cedar closet— Isn't that cedar closet wonderful?"

"What cedar closet?"

"Bill, you didn't see that marvelous cedar closet? You didn't? I'll bet you haven't seen the preserve closet, either. Or the laundry chute. Or the incinerator—"

"Sometimes," Leonidas said, "I think I never shall. Cassie, you get my heavy coat. Dow, you find overshoes. Leslie, will you go out and inform Cuff that I intend to wring his neck if he does not stop blowing the horn of that car? It sounds like feeding time at the zoo. Hurry, please, all of you!"

There was something in the tone of his voice which silenced even Cassie.

While they dashed around, Leonidas strolled into the hallway and consulted the telephone directory.

"Cuff," Leslie reported, "says he just wanted you should get a wiggle on, because there ain't no telling how long it'll take to find Pig Eyes. Look, d'you really think that Chard is the person who killed Medora? Somehow, in spite of everything, I can't seem to convince myself. And d'you think she was trying to explain something to me about her brother? I—"

"Here's your coat," Cassie said. "Smell the cedar. And sit down, and Dow'll put on the overshoes— Dear me, his feet are lots bigger than yours, aren't they? Well, you'll just have to manage—"

Five minutes later, Leonidas managed to cut short her spirited suggestions to Leslie and Dow on the barricading of doors and repelling of boarders, and, with a forceful hand at her elbow, he propelled her down the front walk and into the funereal black sedan.

"Oh, the front seat," Cassie said. "We'll all sit in front. There's loads of room, really. Can you drive all right with your wrist, Cuff?"

"Say," Cuff said, "I could drive this baby with my feet. Shall we go straight halfway up Arthur, huh, Bill?"

"No," Leonidas said. "I want you to circle around the hill—can you? Good. And go to the Winthrop house. Cassie, I don't ever recall your mentioning the name of Winthrop when we talked over my plans for building a house here."

"I probably called it the Blodgett house," Cassie said. "People usually do. The Blodgetts built it. He was a caterer, you know, and I always felt he let one of his pastry cooks design the house on his day off— Why, Bill?"

"The architectural dreams of a pastry cook," Leonidas told her, "are not—er—up my alley, as Cuff might say."

"Why are you going to Medora's?"

"To settle a few problems," Leonidas said, "which rankle. And while I settle them, I expect you to sit quietly in the car, and tell Cuff stories about—well, about the knights of old. Tell him Jock's favorite about

Sir Filbert and Sir Bloot. You might begin now, while I marshal my thoughts."

For all the progress they made, Leonidas decided, his own thoughts might be encased in armor, and rusty armor at that.

"Are you marshaled?" Cassie inquired. "Because here you are. Go ahead and settle problems, if you want to. Cuff, once upon a time, there was a knight—"

Leonidas got out of the car, and walked up the short path from the porte cochère.

He banged the iron knocker and rang the bell, and decided, as he waited for someone to come to the door, that Cassie had erred on the side of restraint in describing Medora Winthrop's house. You could not attribute an edifice like that to one poor pastry cook. Flocks of pastry cooks must have made Blodgett's house their life work.

After listening to the descriptions of Medora Winthrop's servants, Leonidas was prepared to be faced by Jo-Jo, the dog-faced boy. But the door was swung open by a pertly good-looking maid who took one look at Leonidas, and then, with a squeal of pleasure, embraced him soundly.

At the sound of that squeal, Cuff and Cassie came rushing from the car.

"Margie!" Cassie said. "Margie!"

"Aw, Sugar!" Happy tears appeared in Cuff's eyes. "Aw, Sugar, it's you!"

Margie kissed Cuff, kissed Cassie, kissed Leonidas, and then kissed them all over again.

"I've called you," she said at last to Cassie, "every chance I got at the phone, I called your house, but nobody answered all day. Since this morning, I been calling—"

"Sugar," Cuff said, "what you *doin'* here? When'd you come? What you doin' here, huh?"

"Where'd you come from?" Cassie chimed in. "How long have you been here? What on earth are you in this place for?"

"It's all because of Colonel Carpenter," Margie said. "He was at the station this morning— You see, I didn't tell you I was coming home so as to surprise you. Anyway, the colonel was at the station, and he asked me if I'd like to take on a job at twenty-five bucks a day, see, up here at this house. And so—"

"What was Rutherford doing at the station?" Cassie demanded. "Did he know you were coming?"

"Oh, no!" Margie said. "He just happened to see me there at the station. He come to meet a dick."

"Dick who?" Cassie asked.

"A dick," Margie said. "At least he looked like a dick to me. I thought he was a dick when I seen him get on the train last night. Anyway, the colonel sees me at the station, and asks me if I'll help him out and take on a job for the day, so I said sure. He said would I come up here and keep an eye on this Miss Winthrop. And twenty-five bucks," Margie added, "is twenty-five bucks. So I come. I tried to get you on the phone, Mrs. Price, and I tried to get Cuff— Gee, Bill, I never knew you was home, even. Listen, I told the colonel I'd stay here till he comes for me. So you go to Bill's house and wait. I can't let you in here, and I'm freezing to death on this step."

"Say," Cuff said, "was that all you had to do, huh? Just to keep an eye on this old dame that lives here?"

"Yeah. The colonel didn't say why. He said he wanted someone should keep an eye on her, so I come. Listen, I'm frozen. You go along, and I'll meet you at Bill's later. I got to stay here till the old dame gets back."

"But she's dead, Sugar," Cuff said. "The old dame got bumped off in Bill's cellar, see? That's why we're finding out who bumped her off. On account she was bumped off in *his* cellar."

Cuff's tone implied that if Miss Winthrop had been bumped off in anyone else's cellar, it wouldn't have counted.

"Well, for God's sakes!" Margie said. "And me all set to wait up for her! Say, wait till I get my coat!"

Leonidas put out a restraining hand.

"Perhaps you should wait till the colonel comes, Margie."

"Why?" Margie asked simply. "He just told me to keep an eye on her, Bill. And listen, I'm telling you that another ten minutes in this place, and I'd be bats, see? That fish-eyed butler, he's chased me into every corner in this house—"

"Where is the guy?" Cuff demanded ominously. "You show me that guy, Sugar, and I'll hash him!"

"Don't take the trouble, Cuffy," Margie said. "I knocked out his teeth and jumped on 'em. I fixed him. Just you wait till I get my coat—and—gee, I thought of something else. Wait for me in the car till I get those papers."

Five minutes later, Margie scrambled into the sedan.

"Better start it up, Cuffy. That bunch is on my heels asking questions. My God, what a crowd. Here, Bill." She presented him with an envelope. "Maybe these'll do you some good. And say, some dame phoned that Winthrop and this companion of hers was staying in the village for dinner, for that League meeting. Why'd they phone, and say that, if the Winthrop dame's been bumped off?"

"I think," Leonidas said, "that was a rather clever move, Margie, to eliminate any questions that might have arisen in the household concerning Miss Winthrop's continued absence. M'yes. Now, Cuff, if you'll stop by some convenient street light, so that I may read these papers. Why d'you feel they matter, Margie?"

"Winthrop left 'em for her lawyer, see?" Margie said. "That's what I was waiting up in the front hall for, see, to give 'em to the lawyer if he come while the butler and the rest was eating. Say, are they pigs! They just stuff like pigs. I never washed so damn many dishes in my life. All they did was eat, and all I did was work. I figured if she wanted these papers to go to a lawyer, maybe they might help you, Bill. Snap on some light, Cuff, so he can read."

Cuff pressed a button, and the interior of the sedan glowed.

"Rutherford says that Simeon's got everything but running water," Cassie said with pride. "Isn't that a marvelous light? Bill, what are the papers— Why, it's a will! A will, and copies of it! What a short will!"

"Short, simple, and to the point," Leonidas said. "An admirable will, I should say, in every respect."

"To Leslie! She left everything to Leslie!"

"Well, as she points out," Leonidas said, "Leslie Horn was one person who appeared to appreciate her without knowing of her wealth. Asked no favors, and so on and so forth. M'yes. That's substantially the same impression that Dow got. And I must say, I'm delighted that Medora picked Leslie Horn, and not Estelle, or Elsa Otis, for example."

"But, Bill," Cassie said, "Leslie doesn't know anything about this!"

"No," Leonidas agreed, "I don't think Leslie suspected such a thing. Or expected it. But it's all rather obvious, isn't it? Medora is charmed by the girl's letters, she remembers dandling Leslie on her knee, she has happy thoughts of the girl's mother—why not leave Leslie the money?"

"It would explain her asking Leslie here to Dalton, wouldn't it?" Cassie said. "And why she was so upset at Leslie's leaving that way, in such a rush. Perhaps she realized that she hadn't made a good impression on Leslie, what with throwing the clocks at the butler, and all. But, Bill, Chard would have known—no, no, I don't mean about the clocks! Chard would have known about this will—that's it! Chard hoped that Medora would leave everything to her, and when she discovered that Leslie was going to get it all, Chard rose in wrath and killed Medora."

Leonidas pointed out that, under the circumstances, Leslie was the person for Miss Chard to kill. "Not Medora. Snap out the light, will you, Cuff? No, Cassie, Miss Chard would derive no personal benefit from Medora's death. This will seems to be in order. Medora has signed it. So have flocks of witnesses. Medora didn't bother to put it in an envelope, and I've no doubt that the servants have all read it through with care. Killing Medora Winthrop wouldn't benefit Miss Chard. It would only benefit Leslie."

"Does her death have to benefit anyone?" Cassie demanded. "Couldn't she just have been killed, simply because someone wanted to kill her?"

"M'yes," Leonidas said. "But that comes under the heading of homicidal mania, and the average maniac bent on homicide does not usually lure his victim into the garage of a strange house, there to commit his murder with a pickax belonging to the local Chief of Police. A homicidal maniac would be inclined to kill the nearest person with the nearest implement. He would not make elaborate plans which involved my red refrigerator, and the Tuesday Club, and all the rest. In this particular case, considering Medora's wealth, I think it might reasonably be concluded that her murderer anticipated monetary benefit."

"But Leslie didn't even know about this will!" Cassie said. "She didn't know she'd benefit. You just admitted that. Money can't be a motive! And if Medora wasn't just killed—oh, dear, I've never been more confused. Cuff, what d'you think is the motive?"

"Huh?"

"Motive, motive, motive!" Margie said impatiently. "Why do people kill people? You ought to know!"

"Me? Why, Margie, I never killed nobody! That lug in Carnavon looked dead, but it was only his skull got fractured. But if he ever makes another pass at you, Sugar, I'll blot him out. Say, maybe this woman got killed had a boy friend, and maybe she double-crossed him. And—"

"Cuff," Cassie said, "bear in mind that Medora Winthrop was older than I am."

"Oh, was she, huh? Well," Cuff said, "maybe some-one didn't want her to talk, then. The cousin of a guy I know got the chair on account of bumping off four people so as they wouldn't talk. Lots of people get bumped off so as they won't talk. Maybe the old dame knew too much, huh, Bill? Maybe that was it."

"That is an opinion," Leonidas said, "which I per-sonally favor. Medora Winthrop knew too much, and she also had money. Cuff, about this garage on Ar-thur Street. Is it a bona fide establishment? Or is it on the shady side? Is it a—er—joint? I suppose there is a proper term, but I don't know it. Is this a garage where stolen cars are taken?"

Cuff laughed.

"Aw, no, Bill! Didn't I tell you? It's run by a cousin of Rossi's. It's just a garage, like. Gee, Bill,

I'd have known the place if it was a hot car fixery. Say, if *I* din't know about it, it's okay, Bill. And besides that, I know it's okay, anyway."

"Why," Leonidas inquired, "are you so positive, Cuff?"

Cuff laughed again. "Say, Bill, I know every garage in Dalton, see? And Carnavon, and Adamstown, and all abouts. That's why it was so hard remembering about this truck. I knew it was in a place I din't know, see? And besides, I seen all their papers. They're on the square, see? Rossi made me check the papers, see, so nobody wouldn't say he was giving his cousin a break. That's the kind of guy Rossi is, see? Like he said to me, he could have gone through them papers himself, and nobody wouldn't ever of known if he passed over them battery serials or not. But he give the job to me. And they wouldn't of done like that if they hadn't of been on the square. And there was plenty garages, see, that didn't want us to look over their papers and books and stuff. Some of 'em put up an awful squawk."

"Cuff Murray," Margie said, "are you talking about the serial numbers on that battery from the bandit's car?"

"Yeah, sure," Cuff said. "That's when I was in this garage, see. That time when Rossi took me with him while they was checking them battery serials—"

"Cuff!" Cassie said. "Rossi took you to check things?"

"Yeah. You see, Bill," Cuff said with pride, "some guys was trying to hold up the bank, see? And I got the one guy, and the other three, they beat it, and then they ditched the car and burned it, see, and the colonel was trying to track 'em down by the battery. The battery serial number wasn't touched, see? And it was a replacement battery. And we was trying to track it down and find out who bought it, because we found out from the guy that made the batteries it was in a shipment that come to Dalton. But Kelling—that's the guy on Centre Street—bought the lot. He din't keep records who bought 'em off him, on account they was cheap batteries, and wasn't guaranteed, nor nothing. He kept records, but—"

"He kept records," Cassie said, "the way Emory Kelling keeps all records. 'Merchandise, sixteen-eighty-eight.' 'Merchandise, one-thirty-one-ninety-eight.' He might have been selling a battery or a curling iron or a fish rod, for all anyone could tell from his old records! Rutherford said he understood perfectly why Emory Kelling was always in hot water with the Income Tax Department, and always being fined. Anyway, Rutherford took all those bills for merchandise that month, and tried to find out which one might have been for that battery, and who bought it, and who *he* sold it to. D'you see?"

"M'yes," Leonidas said. "Rutherford would take, for example, John Smith's bill for eighteen dollars, and try to find out from John Smith what the merchandise might have been."

"Yes—how well you put things, Bill! And of course, most of the garages and the electrical men and everyone who bought from Kelling's had their own records," Cassie said, "showing just what the items were that they bought. Rutherford managed to track down every last battery except one, that one. And I begin to see why. Look, Cuff, Rossi actually took you with him to this Arthur Street garage, and made you check the books, and the vouchers?"

"Huh?"

"The books! The vouchers! The duplicates! The stubs! The counterfoils! The—oh, what's the use." Cassie said, "What *is* the use? You don't even know what I'm talking about! Margie, did you have any inkling of this?"

"He never said a word, the dope. I know all about the bandit he got, but I never heard a murmur about this. The dope! Cuff, you lump!"

"Aw—"

"From now on," Margie said, "you better just tell

me everything, see? Bill, is this mixed up with this Winthrop dame?"

"Remotely," Leonidas said. "M'yes. I begin to see things. Cuff, you had your picture taken helping kiddies cross streets, so I assume that you're regularly assigned to a prowl car. Are you?"

"Car Twenty," Cuff said. "But that was a special detail, see? Rossi took me special. It made a nice change. I liked it."

"Oh, Cuff!" Cassie said. "Why didn't you tell me, or Margie!"

"I told you I had a special detail one day," Cuff protested. "I did tell you."

"But it was on Washington's Birthday, wasn't it?" Cassie said. "Back then? I just naturally thought it was the parade detail! Oh, Cuff, and you don't even know a voucher from an ostrich! Could you understand anything that you read?"

"Aw, sure, Mrs. Price! Rossi gimme the papers," Cuff said, "and I sat down at the desk, and I read through all of 'em. It wasn't very hard. Honest. They was all typed, see, in big print. Like you done the exam answers I learned—"

"I knew," Leonidas said, "that sooner or later that would come out. Cassie, you stole the police examination papers, didn't you?"

"Why, Bill, I never did!" Cassie said righteously.

"What a malicious thought! Jock just happened to be in the room while Rutherford was making out the questions, and purely by chance—by the remotest chance, Bill, Jock spilled the ink on the question paper, and then, naturally, he offered to type the paper over for Rutherford. And—"

"And you took the ink-stained paper," Leonidas said, "and typed out the answers, and taught them to Cuff!"

"Jock said you'd find out," Cassie said. "He knew you would. My, what a week! It was like trying to teach Eliza to talk properly in *Pygmalion*. Jock and Margie and I had to take that Jamaica cruise to rest up. We were awfully afraid Rutherford might change the order of the questions, but mercifully, he didn't. And really, Cuff's done a lot of *good* since he got on the force—"

"M'yes," Leonidas said drily. "Safeguarding the kiddies, and encouraging his ex-pals to—er—swipe the seventh hole. Cuff, what are we slowing down for?"

"That car, Bill," Cuff said. "We din't shake it off, just circling the hill."

"What car?" Margie demanded. "Cuff, you big dope, *what* car?"

"The car," Cuff explained patiently, "that's been trailing us since we left Bill's place. *That* car."

CHAPTER VIII

"A CAR trailing us, since we left the hill, since we left Bill's?" Cassie made a little squealing sound. "A car? Trailing us?"

"Yeah. We din't shake it off just circling the hill. That was what you circled the hill for, wasn't it, Bill?"

"Frankly, no," Leonidas said. "I told you to circle the hill so that we would approach the Winthrop house from the left, and make it appear to any of the servants who might be watching that we had come from the village. I admit thinking that someone might try to enter my house, but it never entered my head that anyone would follow us."

"Aw, din't you?" Cuff sounded as though he were disappointed in Leonidas. "Gee, I thought you tumbled right off. I seen that car park off the corner while we was at the Winthrop house, but I thought it was only the prowl car, see? I didn't really notice till it slowed down when I slowed down for you to read the will later. It slows when I slow, see, and it picks up when I do, and I twisted around North Main, and it did too, and it's hanging right along. See?" he indicated the rear-vision mirror. "It just jumped the car that swung in behind us off North Cedar. They're trailing us, all right."

"Can't you shake them?" Cassie demanded.

Cuff smiled.

"In this baby," he said, "I can shake anything in this world. Just you watch. I'll run you down the loop, and then through the old car barns, and then by the viaduct—"

"Wait," Leonidas said, as Cuff's foot started to press down on the accelerator. "Wait. Before you—"

"Wait for what?" Cassie said. "You don't want to be followed, do you?"

"No, I don't. On the other hand—"

"People don't follow people," Cassie said ominously, "for any good! You can't tell what someone might be planning to do to us. Why, think of Haseltine! Someone in Haseltine is always being forced to the side of the road in a car, and being hurtled over some precipice! Think of when Casimir edged Lady Peggy over that awful ravine! Why, Bill, you just can't tell what people are up to when they trail you in cars!"

"True," Leonidas said. "But I like to think, Cassie, that people are following us because they are faintly puzzled. If they'd intended to harm us, they passed by any number of excellent opportunities coming down the hill. No, I think that people merely wish to know what we are doing. I don't like being followed, but on the other hand, as I started to say, I should like to know who is following us. I have what amounts to a burning passion to know the occupants of that car. Er—instead of jeopardizing our lives rushing through car barns and viaducts, Cuff, would it be possible for you to ascertain the identity of our pursuers, and then depart from them in some less spectacular fashion?"

"Huh?"

"Bill wants to find out who's trailing us," Margie translated, "and then beat it. Can you do it, Cuffy?"

"Gee, I guess so," Cuff said. "Only most usually I just always beat it, Sugar."

"Suppose," Leonidas said, "you were to pull into a parking space— I wonder if any are cleared?"

"The one by the auditorium is," Cassie informed him. "They were clearing it this morning. But if we pull into a parking space, they'll just wait till we pull out, or else follow us on foot."

"Listen," Leonidas said, "very carefully. Let's see if this won't work. Listen hard, Cuff."

Cassie gurgled with pleasure as he unfolded his plan, and added a suggestion of her own which inspired Margie to add another.

"Fine," Leonidas said. "Now, you circle around the auditorium block as though you were hunting a parking space, stopping and then starting up again. Got that, Cuff?"

"He gets it," Margie said. "He's awful quick at things you do. It's just things you think that floor him. When we come to the old high school, Cuff gives me the wheel, and crawls out, by the east side of the parking lot."

"Then," Cassie said, "we circle the block again, while Cuff watches this car following us, sees who's in it, and gets the plate numbers. On our second circle, he checks up and makes sure, and we pull into the parking space, and leave the car in front of that little house where the attendants stay, and we go in."

Some eight minutes later, Cassie and Margie bustled out of the door marked "Women" at the rear of the attendant's little house, while Leonidas strolled out of the door marked "Men."

"It's awfully lucky I knew about these doors," Cassie said as the trio met and hurried towards the back of the parking lot. "Because if you watched us go in that place, you'd think we'd gone to the phone booths. I'd never have known if I hadn't lost Estelle and Hattie and Ernest one day— Isn't this working nicely?"

"It is," Leonidas said, "if Cuff has managed to do his part."

"Oh, he'll have a car," Margie assured him. "He always does."

"He's wonderful," Cassie said. "Rutherford can't believe that Cuff does it with that little gadget. Rutherford says it's black magic, and he never saw anything like it outside of Haiti. It just doesn't make any difference what's locked. Cuff just takes that little gadget, and—see, there he is! What a nice car!"

Calmly, as though it were her invariable custom to ride in hastily pilfered cars, Cassie opened the door of the smart sedan and got in.

"Hurry, Bill, hurry, Margie," she said. "Cuff, what a nice car! I wish Simeon had such a pretty instrument panel!"

"Aw," Cuff said, "if that chauffeur hadn't come back for his ear muffs, I'd of got you a Cadillac Sixteen. Say, Bill, I'm sore. I'm plenty sore. Margie, I'm sore."

"I'm sure," Leonidas said, "this car will do as well as the Cadillac. The heater is admirable. You needn't be sore that you were thwarted about the Sixteen—"

"Aw, it ain't that, Bill. That ain't what I'm sore about. Say, you know who it was trailing us, huh?"

Leonidas nodded.

"Your friend Rossi, was it not?"

"Say!" Cuff turned a corner on half a wheel. "Say, how'd you know, huh?"

"I guessed," Leonidas said. "Was there anyone with him?"

"Yeah. That guy. His cousin. The garage one. Say, Bill, I been getting a free ride, ain't I?"

"If you mean," Leonidas said gently, "that Rossi has been deliberately misleading you, yes. I'm quite sure he has been."

"Telling me all the time how much he liked the colonel!" Cuff said. "On account of he knew I'd most likely tell Mrs. Price. And he picks me to check on that battery serial because he knew I—aw, gee! And I been reading all the books Jock give me, and all! Honest, I never caught on!"

Leonidas stepped on Margie's foot.

"After all, Cuff," he was afraid that Cuff was going to burst into tears, "Rossi knew you weren't used to clerical work. After all, clerical work is not your forte. Er—don't you think that's so, Cassie?"

"I think that's as nice a phrase," Cassie said, "as you ever coined. Ssh, Margie! Bill's right. Rossi knew Cuff wasn't used to clerical work, so he picked him to wade through a lot of faked papers. You hadn't done any other checking, had you? Well, Rossi knew you hadn't. He knew he could fool you easier than he could fool some of the others who were used to clerical work."

"You think," Cuff said, "he picked me because I

don't know about papers, and not on account of I don't read very good?"

"I'm sure of it," Leonidas said promptly. "And tell me, Cuff, what made you catch on to them so quickly now?"

Cuff brightened.

"Well, they was trailing us, all right. They was the ones. And then the car they got. Phony plates, see? Fixed plates. I can spot 'em a mile away. And it's a quick repaint job—"

"You mean they're in a stolen car?" Cassie said.

"Yeah. And then their clothes— I never seen Rossi out of uniform before, see? And the time I seen the cousin, he was in overalls and all grease, see? Gee, I'm dumb! But I bet you the colonel's caught on. Every morning for a week when I reported at the station, see, the colonel's called me in and showed me pictures, and asked if any of the guys looked like them guys got away, see? And this morning, it did. They had hats on, and the brims snapped down—and it was the same around the mouth. Just like them two now!"

"I was right!" Cassie said. "I was right! Rutherford *is* on the trail of something about Rossi, and that's why Feeny acted that way. Feeny goes through the mail, doesn't he, Cuff? And the pictures that get sent from the other police departments. Oh, my, how nicely it's beginning to fit!"

"And the—er—dick at the station," Leonidas said. "Things are fitting. Cuff, where are we?"

"Oh, I'm just weaving around West Dalton," Cuff said. "They din't spot us. Shall I go to the garage now?"

"Frankly," Leonidas said, "I don't feel there's much use. But some day you must find out what happened to Pig Eyes."

"What do you mean?" Cassie stared at him. "What happened to him?"

Leonidas smiled.

"I feel, Cassie, that Pig Eyes has gone on a long, long journey of one description or another. It ought to be easy to find out. Cuff, wouldn't someone at Dinty's know?"

"In town a day," Cuff said wonderingly, "and already you know about Dinty's!"

"M'yes. Remind me to give you a card," Leonidas said, "entitling you to a free evening of bowling. Stop at this drugstore ahead, and phone Dinty's, and ask the bartender— You know him, don't you?"

"Say," Cuff said, "Dinty's my own cousin! Say, whyn't I think to call him right off? That would of been a cinch!"

"M'yes," Leonidas said, "we did rather choose the hard way, didn't we? But we found out a great deal more. Hurry, Cuff."

Cuff vaulted a snow bank and disappeared into the drugstore.

"The dope!" Margie said. "The poor, sweet dope! He feels terrible, Mrs. Price. Well, I guess I learned my lesson. I guess I don't leave him alone again, ever."

"He's tried so hard," Cassie said. "Mostly I think he hates to feel that he's let Rutherford down. He adores Rutherford. Bill, the Voters League."

"M'yes."

"They'll put that Scipione up for mayor, and Ward Four'll elect him on the strength of the clambakes and the free milk and the Beano. Rossi'll take over the police. Rutherford'll be out on his ear, which doesn't largely matter, but the Police Department will be crooked, and that does matter. All those women, Bill. Think of 'em. Hattie and Estelle and all the rest of Tudbury's Horse, all rushing around getting money for the Voters League, and Clean Government for Dalton. Digging their graves with their teeth—no, that's not the one I mean. Hoist with their own petard. Anyway, you know what I'm driving at."

"M'yes," Leonidas said again.

"Sometimes I wonder," Cassie said, "if a woman's place isn't in the home! Sometimes I think women should stay right in their own kitchens, mashing potatoes and scouring pans!"

Leonidas did not answer. Neither he nor Margie

pointed out that Cassie rarely mashed potaoes or scoured pans, herself.

"Anyway," Cassie went on, "they ought to stay home more. Think of Jock. If his mother isn't skiing on pine needles, she's skiing on snow, and in between times, she goes to lectures about the dictatorship of the proletariat. You should see Jock's socks."

"Jock doesn't seem to suffer," Leonidas remarked.

"No, but he has perspective," Cassie said. "He looks on the proletariat and the skiing with the same detachment his grandfather looked on my suffragettes and the Camping Club. Jock's very like his grandfather. But look at Elsa— Oh, Bill, this hasn't anything to do with Medora, except that I was right, wasn't I, when I said we simply couldn't let Rossi take charge of things?"

"Subsequent events," Leonidas said, "seem to bear out your contention that Rossi was not the ideal person to be summoned— Ah, Cuff. What of Pig Eyes?"

Cuff climbed in behind the wheel.

"Bill, I take my hat off to you! Pig Eyes—his real name's Binsky, or something. Well, he come to Dinty's at five minutes of three this after, see, and he has three slugs of gin, and he takes the three-o'clock Providence bus. Dinty says he couldn't hardly wait for the bus to leave the corner. Here."

He emptied a fistful of quarters into Margie's lap.

"Cuff," Cassie said severely, "you stopped to play the slot machine, didn't you? And you promised Margie and me!"

"You promised us," Margie said. "You swore that you wouldn't touch another slot machine! After you lost all that money on Marlene, you promised—"

"Yeah, Sugar Pie," Cuff said. "I know. But this was different. I says to myself, if I hit it, that's a good sign, see? That means Bill finds out who done it, and I get to knock that guy's block off. And I hit it, and you can keep the jackpot for the bank book. And it means everything's going to come out fine, see? Don't you think it's a good sign?" He appealed to Leonidas. "Ain't it a good sign?"

"It is rather a far cry," Leonidas said, "from the examination of—er—bovine viscera to the examination of the entrails of a slot machine, but I suppose one might still term it haruspication. M'yes. It is heartening to know that the Fates look kindly on us. Cuff, will you be good enough to take us, please, to Fourteen Florence Street? I want to inquire after George."

Cassie eyed him with suspicion.

"I always thought haruspication was geese honking," she said. "And I don't intend to be caught again. Is it George Street, or George Alley, or George Court? George What?"

"George Chard," Leonidas told her. "And geese honking is augury, Cassie. Haruspication involves viscera. Of course, if it happened to involve the viscera of geese, I've no doubt they honked to a considerable extent, but—"

"How d'you know that George Chard lives at Fourteen Florence Street?" Cassie interrupted.

"I have practically never found reason," Leonidas said, "to question the listings in a telephone directory. If the telephone company says that George Chard—he is Dalton's only Chard, by the way—if they say he lives at Fourteen Florence, I accept that fact as gospel truth. There is, of course, the possibility that George may have moved, but I think not. My telephone directory is a very recent telephone directory—"

"You found him in the phone book!" Cassie said. "Bill, you're just so smart! But what do you mean, inquire after him?"

"Miss Chard told Leslie that George is a musician," Leonidas said. "I think we may assume that George is not a particularly prosperous musician, if he lives on Florence Street. And you remember that George went out without his overshoes. And since that fact loomed so important, I think we may further assume that George, in his overshoeless state, took cold. In fact, I think that George became seriously ill. Doubtless the poor fellow was in a run-down condition."

"If you want to know," Cassie said, "*I* am practically in a run-down condition, myself! Bill, d'you *feel* all right? Maybe there's carbon monoxide coming out of that heater. Cuff, perhaps we'd better leave this car and take another. Bill's being affected by the heater fumes."

"Heater fumes," Leonidas said, "are probably the only thing not affecting my condition, but I agree that a change of cars is indicated. I should not care, at this point, to be detained by the police for being an occupant of a stolen car. And it's about time someone reported this. Possibly we might take a taxi."

Cassie and Cuff looked horror-stricken at his suggestion. Margie sniffed.

"Aw, no, Bill!" Cuff said. "You can't! Why, the colonel's hand-picked the cab drivers, Bill. They ain't the way they used to be. Say, if you get a cab, and you get chased, they'd let you get *caught!*"

"Absolutely!" Cassie said. "A cab would be fatal. Why, suppose we'd been in a cab coming from your house! We shouldn't have known we were being followed, and the Lord only knows what mightn't have happened to us at that awful garage place halfway up Arthur!"

"Wow!" Cuff said. "If we'd gone there! Say, they'd

be picking us up in pieces out of a Carnavon ditch tomorrow!"

"Very well." Leonidas gave in. "Get another car, Cuff."

"It's the best thing, Bill. I'll swing around by the movies. There's always plenty of cars outside the movies, and if you get one from somebody just going in, then nobody reports it for a couple hours. I'll get a nice snappy roadster. I like snappy open jobs."

Margie reminded him of the weather.

"Below zero, dopey, and you talk about open jobs! Listen, you get a nice sedan with a heater!"

"And nothing conspicuous, please," Leonidas added. "Something commonplace, that won't call attention to us. Something quiet. No chromium."

"Aw," Cuff said, "while I'm about it, I might as well get a good one!"

"Something quiet."

Cuff sighed.

"Okay. I'll get you a plain sedan. Gee, if we was over by the Centre—"

"You'd what?" Margie demanded, as Cuff hesitated.

"Aw, I just got a thought," Cuff said. "I know just the car." A dreamy look flitted over his face. "It'd do swell. I could get it— Say, where'll I leave you? I better leave you somewheres while I get something. How's for I leave you to wait at a bus stop, huh?"

"Not in this cold!" Cassie said. "We're not going to freeze in one of those lean-tos. Where are we, in Daltonham? Well, turn down the avenue and leave us at the railroad station. At least it'll be warm."

Margie got out with Leonidas and Cassie at the station, and then she climbed back in the car beside Cuff.

"I think," she said, "I'll stay with him. I think I better look after him. We'll be right back."

"I think," Cassie said as the car sped away, "that she guessed it, too. Bill, that boy's got something up his sleeve. I do hope she stops him."

"She will," Leonidas said. "I have the utmost faith in Margie."

"Yes, but when Cuff gets an idea," Cassie said, "he's terribly inclined to cling to it. Think how long he clung to the notion that Rossi was a fine fellow. Well, it's up to Margie. Bill, do you really think that Chard had nothing to do with Pig Eyes, and that garage, and trying to get your red refrigerator? Do you think she was just going to see her sick brother? You really do? Then, why did she run away from Dow, and yell 'Stop thief!' and all?"

"Suppose that you were walking alone down one of Dalton's less reputable streets on a cold, dark March evening," Leonidas said. "Suppose you realized that you were being followed. D'you think you'd pause to discover the gentleman's identity, or d'you think you'd do just what Miss Chard did? Er—if you recall, flight was your impulse when Cuff said we were being trailed, just now."

"I suppose," Cassie said, "that you're right. Do you think she'll be there on Florence Street now?"

"If she's not there, someone will know where she may be found. And I do want," Leonidas said, "to find out how much money Medora kept in the brush box."

Cassie looked wildly around the station's waiting room.

"Bill, I can't scream in here! I simply can't! Tell me quickly what you're talking about! Who ever said one word about Medora keeping money in a box! What box? What money?"

"D'you remember what Miss Chard took from Leslie on the train?"

"The gun and the handcuffs," Cassie said, "the hundred-dollar bill, and the brush box. But—"

"M'yes," Leonidas said. "But, when Leslie so hurriedly left Medora's house yesterday, she had only the brush box in her possession. The gun and the handcuffs, and the hundred-dollar bill were all acquired after she got to New York. Therefore, we may conclude that the brush box was the item which mattered. Er—d'you know what a brush box is like?"

"I know what a brush is," Cassie returned, "and I know what a box is, but until today I never knew that a brush box existed!"

"It's a longish, narrow tin box," Leonidas explained, "with a tightly fitting hinged lid. Once, many years ago, I made a bicycle tour of England with a friend who was addicted to water colors, and I spent a large portion of the time breaking my thumbnails in an effort to open that infernal brush box for him. In short, a brush box makes an excellent receptacle in which to keep things, and you can be sure that the things won't fall out."

"But Medora—"

"Medora," Leonidas said, "liked to keep things in boxes. Dow established that fact. She enjoyed keeping valuable things in boxes. She hoarded bills in boxes. In the library of her house she had an old-fashioned safe which, I gather, a child could open."

"With roses," Cassie said. "Jock did. He was just fiddling with it, one day while we were waiting to take Medora to a committee meeting, and it popped open."

"M'yes. And I like to think," Leonidas said, "that Medora kept in that safe a brush box containing money—"

"I've never felt so Columbus-and-the-eggy in my life," Cassie said. "Of course! After Leslie left, Medora found she'd been robbed! Someone swiped her brush box full of bills. And so she sent Chard after Leslie, to see whether Leslie had swiped it, or whether Leslie had her own brush box full of brushes, or whether it was all a mix-up of brush boxes, or what not. And—why, that was why she had the will! She was waiting to see if Leslie was the thief before she destroyed it! But she didn't!"

"Exactly," Leonidas said. "The brush box which Miss Chard brought to Medora this morning was Leslie's own brush box, filled with brushes. The hundred-dollar bill, as they doubtless discovered from their check list, or from the bank's check list, was not one of the missing bills. So Medora knew that Leslie was not the thief. She didn't destroy the will. She telephoned a lawyer to come and get it."

"Why didn't Medora tell Rutherford?" Cassie said. "Why didn't she tell the police?"

Leonidas smiled.

"Think," he said.

"Bill! You mean that Medora was killed before she could tell! But why did she wait? This must have happened yesterday! Chard got to New York last night in time to take the midnight. She must have left here yesterday evening! Medora must have known yesterday afternoon— Why did she wait?"

"Medora," Leonidas said, "was making sure. It was

either Leslie, who left so hurriedly, or it was X. She waited until she was able to satisfy herself about Leslie—after all, she didn't know the girl. Then—"

"Then she went bounding off in the Birch Hill bus to the lecture-luncheon!" Cassie said. "Oh, Bill, that's silly. If she knew it was either Leslie or X, and she proved it wasn't Leslie, then she knew it was X. Didn't she? Well, under the circumstances, she wouldn't go to the Tuesday Club's lecture-luncheon! Not if I know Medora, she wouldn't! She'd set right out on the trail of X!"

"M'yes." Leonidas put on his pince-nez and looked out of the window. "M'yes. And so she did, Cassie. So she did."

The noise of a passing freight train mercifully drowned out Cassie's scream.

"She went to the lecture-lunch, and she was on the trail of X? Bill, d'you mean Medora was killed by a woman? Someone in the Tuesday Club?"

"Sometimes," Leonidas said, "sometimes I wonder about you, Cassie. Sometimes you know so much about women that you appal me, and then again you ignore the most obvious feminine touches!"

"I do not consider a pickax a feminine touch!" Cassie said indignantly. "Very few women know anything about pickaxes. I can't think of a single woman in the Tuesday Club who ever swung a pickax!"

"Who but a woman," Leonidas said, "would take it for granted that anyone would willingly and gladly and unhesitatingly exchange a refrigerator for a bigger one, a better one, or a newer one? If a man likes something, he is not going to be lured into giving it up for something bigger and better!"

"Why, I know that!" Cassie said. "You should have seen the clothes that Bagley used to fish in. That hat! I bought him a thousand hats, but he still wore that awful thing—oh. Oh, that's what you mean, isn't it? Well, there you are, right back to Chard. She never married. She probably doesn't know— Bill, what are you grinning at?"

"The hats," Leonidas said. "Even you, Cassie!"

"Well," Cassie said, "you still can't get away from Chard by laughing at me! You can't justify her actions. You can't justify her throwing away the gun and handcuffs, and knocking Leslie out, and biffing you, and rushing around your house this morning!"

"I think so," Leonidas said. "Suppose that Miss Chard felt, all along, that Leslie stole Medora's brush box—"

"Why?"

"Why not? The girl left in a rush, without explanations, and the money was gone. Anyway, when Miss Chard found that hundred-dollar bill in Leslie's pocketbook, she was probably very sure that Leslie was the thief. When she found the gun and handcuffs, she was probably positive. And I've no doubt she felt, also, that she was dealing with a thoroughly hardened criminal."

"But the gun didn't work. The handcuffs were locked. You knew it. You said so!"

"M'yes, but I wonder," Leonidas said, "if Chard would have had sufficient experience with guns and handcuffs to know. Would you have known at once, Cassie? Would you have thought to investigate? Would it ever have occurred to you that the gun and handcuffs were to be used as models for a toothpaste advertisement?"

"Never," Cassie said. "You're right, Bill."

"I think so. Now, Miss Chard's orders were to bring Leslie back to Medora in Dalton. I suppose she thought the chances of getting her there intact would be greater if the gun and handcuffs were erased from the scene."

"But why put them in a water cooler?"

"There were double windows on the Pullman," Leonidas pointed out. "Chard wouldn't know how to open a vestibule door. If you pause and reflect, you'll agree with me that she did the best she could in disposing of them. Then, on her return to the drawing room, Leslie pounced on her—"

"What was that Leslie said?" Cassie interrupted.

"Something about threatening her with every known form of torture?"

"M'yes. Suppose you had been in Chard's place," Leonidas said. "What would you have thought?"

"I should have been beyond thought," Cassie returned. "Bill, I don't understand how you can be so convincing about something you're just guessing at from start to finish. But try and explain why you were knocked out. And how she expected to get Leslie off the train, after knocking *her* out!"

"Probably, after seeing me by the water cooler," Leonidas said blandly, "Chard jumped to the conclusion that I was Leslie's accomplice. And I assume she intended to explain Leslie by insinuating that the girl was mentally deranged, and in her care. Something like that."

"Don't you suppose she thought Leslie would have something to say?" Cassie demanded. "She certainly wouldn't be fool enough to expect that Leslie would take something like that without a murmur!"

"That's where the gun and the handcuffs come in," Leonidas said. "Chard knew that Leslie, after her trip to the water cooler, would undoubtedly have the gun and handcuffs with her. Leslie had probably made it very clear that she intended to get them. So that is why Miss Chard was waiting to knock Leslie out with the heel of the—er—arch supporter."

Cassie stared at him.

"Ground gripper. Bill, you mean that Chard was going to take the gun, and force Leslie to do whatever she wanted, at gunpoint. And then Chard found out that the gun wasn't loaded, and no good, and all!"

"I think so," Leonidas said. "I think, for a few unhappy moments before I appeared on the scene, that Miss Chard succumbed utterly to panic. I think she had cleared up the drawing room, and pulled down the shades, and arranged the blankets on top of Leslie's inert form with the intention of leaving her and retiring from the whole affair. I think that Miss Chard was calling quits when I came in."

He brushed his hand across the steamed window pane, and once again peered out.

"You make it all sound so awfully logical!" Cassie said. "I don't like to carp, but your story of what happened on the train was fantastic, and so was Leslie's. How can you make this sound so logical?"

Leonidas admitted that his own version of the train episode made little sense in itself.

"Nor did Leslie's. But when you add my story to hers, things take form."

"You've certainly made them take form! Hm," Cassie said, "I suppose, when Chard found out the gun was no good, she nearly went out of her mind. I would have. And that's why she biffed you. And why she jumped at Leslie's suggestion that they get out, and why she thought of the Carnavon train, and all. I'd have chinned myself from a straw to get out of the hole she was in. Bill, I must say that Chard has a strong sense of duty."

"M'yes. Quite."

"The strongest sense of duty I ever heard of. To go through all that because Medora told her to! It's incredible. But that's probably what she was trying to explain to Leslie while they waited to get off at Back Bay. About how she was just doing her duty —Bill, don't you see any signs of Cuff and Margie? Where can those two be? I'm getting worried!"

"I'll give them five minutes more," Leonidas said, "and then we will take a cab. What time is it, eight-thirty? Ah, yes. I suppose it only seems later. But, Cassie, Miss Chard didn't mean her duty to Medora. She meant her duty to her poor brother George. You know," he swung his pince-nez impatiently, "I've never in all my life been as utterly thwarted as I've been today, Cassie. Just one thwart, as you might say, after another. Now I can't even get to inquire after poor sick George Chard, without being delayed, and thwarted."

"It's the heater fumes," Cassie said promptly. "They've affected you. Sit down here on the bench,

Bill, and let me get you a nice drink of water. George is *Chard's* brother, you know. It was *Medora* that Chard was doing her duty to."

"Cassie," Leonidas said, "would you have gone through with any such expedition simply because Medora Winthrop ordered you to?"

"Certainly not," Cassie said. "I should have told her that I was a companion-housekeeper-secretary, but I drew the line at tracking down thieves. You'd have to draw the line somewhere."

"Unless, possibly," Leonidas said, "you wished to exonerate yourself. Suppose that with your poor brother George ill, you helped yourself to a small amount of Medora's money. And then suppose someone else took the entire sum. That would be a sufficient goad for you to fly after Leslie, wouldn't it? Because, whereas Medora would give money to Rutherford for a new pistol range, I doubt if she'd lend him carfare. Medora wouldn't lend me carfare. She wouldn't lend money to anyone."

"That's perfectly true," Cassie said. "She never lent a cent in her life. Not even ferry toll, that time I forgot my pocketbook. I had to borrow from the toll man. She'd never have lent Chard a cent, or advanced her a penny of her salary. She was like that. She—but see here, Bill, how do you know that? Bill, you knew Medora!"

"M'yes," Leonidas said. "Didn't you guess? I knew her when she was young, and not unlike Elsa Otis. Not," he added critically, "not quite so many teeth, perhaps, but otherwise she was very like Elsa. And, like Dow, somehow I found myself engaged to Medora."

"And you jilted her!" Cassie said. "You'd had to have. She'd never have let you go. That's why she was so rabid about you, and why she was going to run you out of town—oh, of course! We always called you Bill, or Bill Shakespeare, and we called your house 'Bill's place.' And then she found out it was you. Was that why you made that crack about being in the cobra's grasp?"

Leonidas nodded.

"I began to realize the possibilities of the situation. Er—'Bearded Swain Slays Former Jilted Fiancee with Police Chief's Ax.' That sort of thing."

"How'd you ever manage to jilt her?" Cassie asked interestedly. "What happened? Quick—is that Cuff and Margie?"

"Just a taxi circling around. Frankly," Leonidas said with a reminiscent smile, "I was pretty despondent about Medora. Jilting was harder in those days. Then, one night, I recklessly took her home from a concert in a carriage, all the way to Melrose. And after I paid the driver and sent him off, I discovered that I hadn't train fare back to Boston. So, rather shamefacedly, I asked Medora—"

"And she got furious!"

"She slammed the door in my face," Leonidas said, "and I walked home. The next afternoon I called to apologize, and to beg the loan of fifty dollars. That, I am happy to say, terminated our engagement."

Cassie grinned.

"No wonder she didn't want you perched up alongside her, on the hill. Hell hath no fury like a woman scorned. Of course, you didn't exactly scorn her."

"No," Leonidas said, "but it amounted to the same thing. I think possibly that explains why Miss Chard was wandering around this morning. She probably told Medora all that happened on the train, and described me."

"And Medora sent her over to see if you were well enough to be brought home, or to come home. Bill, I simply never heard anything like this. Nothing happens. Like Haseltine, I mean. No one's been dynamited, or dropped from an airplane, but it just seems to be getting more and more complicated every single minute!"

"On the contrary," Leonidas said, "it is boiling itself down. All I really want to know, now, is how much money was in the brush box. If it's a sufficiently large sum, I think we may well uphold Cuff's—er—haruspication, and say that everything will be settled quite soon."

Cassie gritted her teeth.

"I keep asking myself," she said plaintively, "*is it those heater fumes, or does he really know! Do you? And what about your red refrigerator, Bill? What's that got to do with it? Why—Bill, there's a car! Is it them? Look and see!"

Leonidas looked, and then reached for his hat.

"Lieutenant Haseltine," he said, "was never any gladder to see the U.S.S. *Idaho* steam into sight over the horizon. Come along!"

The two of them rushed out of the station.

"That's a nice enough sedan," Cassie said, "but why it took him all this time to get it— Bill, look! Look!"

But Leonidas was already aware of Miss Chard, shivering on the seat beside Cuff and Margie.

CHAPTER IX

"SWISS CHARD! Swiss—"

"Stop, Cassie," Leonidas said firmly. "We had enough of that this afternoon!"

"But it's Miss Chard. It *is*, isn't it?" Cassie climbed into the sedan. "It is you, isn't it, Miss Chard?"

"Yes." Miss Chard didn't sound any too positive, Leonidas thought. She sounded frightened to death. "Mrs. Price, this young fellow and this young woman have kept saying that I'd see you and talk with you, and—oh, I'm upset! They kept saying that if I'd just wait, you'd explain everything. But I don't understand. Any of it. I don't understand a bit!"

"Nobody does," Cassie returned. "Only Bill, and he's just guessing. Where'd they find you?"

"I was just walking into the auditorium—for the monster Voters League meeting, you know. I hadn't intended to go, but Mrs. Otis said I must, because it was very important. And as I went up the steps, a man came up and asked if I were Miss Chard, and I said yes, and he said that a lady wanted to see me.

So I followed him, and there was another man stand-ing beside a car, and then this young man here—is his name Duff?"

"Cuff. Call him anything," Cassie said, "but get on!"

"He came along, and then," Miss Chard said un-happily, "there was a fight. It all happened so quickly, I couldn't tell *what* went on. It was so dark, out there."

"Who, Cuff?" Leonidas demanded. "Rossi, and his cousin? Margie, what went on?"

"It was Rossi and his pal," Margie said. "They were just going to take her for a ride in this car."

"Is this Rossi's car?" Cassie said. "*This?*"

"Of course it's Rossi's," Leonidas told her. "Cuff had 'Rossi's car' written in large letters on his fore-head when he left us at the station. I knew he couldn't resist taking it sooner or later. So Rossi and his cousin were about to take Miss Chard for a ride when you intervened. M'yes. I should have thought—"

"Not for a ride," Miss Chard said. "I'm afraid you've misunderstood. Some woman wished to see me."

Margie sighed.

"You don't know what we been up against, Bill," she said. "She still doesn't know what she almost walked into!"

"Where are Rossi and the cousin now?" Leonidas asked. "What did you do with them?"

"They're okay," Cuff said. "And, say, Bill, my wrist's all right. Ain't that a joke on the doc, huh?"

"*Where!*" Leonidas said. "What did you do with them?"

"Oh, we left 'em up at your house," Cuff said. "The wrist don't hurt a bit, Bill. And it's still got the old snap—"

"Margie," Leonidas said, "did he knock out Rossi and the cousin, and take them to my house? Clear this up, quickly!"

"That's right, Bill. There was a Camera Club taking pictures of your living room, but Dow and that girl was looking out for everything all right. Rossi and the cousin are down in the cellar hall. They're safe—"

"I'll say they're safe," Cuff interrupted happily. "Rossi's got a busted jaw, and the other guy's got a busted nose. And besides I left the twins there to look after 'em. I picks up the twins, see, outside the hall. They was there with a bunch from Ward Four. All set to demonstrate—"

"All we lacked," Leonidas said, "were twins. What twins? Margie, whose twins?"

"Cuff's twin brothers, Bill," Margie explained. "Biff and Bat. They're standing guard. Everything's okay up

there. That Camera Club didn't see us. We went in
the back way. We had sort of trouble with her," she
pointed to Miss Chard, "so I thought we'd better
bring her along to you and let you explain before she
talked to the wrong people. Say, at this auditorium
meeting, they're going—"

"Wait," Cassie said. "Miss Chard, I want to ask
you something. I'm going to ask her, Bill, and if she
answers the right way, I'll believe you. I mean, I'll believe you know what you're talking about, and it's
not heater fumes. Miss Chard," Cassie paused and
drew a long breath, "how much money was there in
the brush box that was stolen from Medora's safe
yesterday afternoon?"

"Forty-two thousand, six hundred and four dollars,
seventy-three cents," Miss Chard said precisely. "I
told her it was too much to keep in the house, but
you know how she loves to keep money around, and
besides, she was going to buy a car."

"Lady," Cuff looked at Miss Chard with reverent
interest, "what kind of bus was you going to buy for
that?"

"Oh, you've misunderstood me again," Miss Chard
said. "It wasn't to be a bus. And of course it wouldn't
cost all that. But with a car, there will be no need for
the bus stop, so Medora sold her Transit Company

holdings. That's how there happened to be so much money, you see. She insists always on cash payments, after that broker who swindled her in twenty-nine."

"And how much," Cassie gulped, "did you need for George?"

"Only a hundred dollars. I paid it back this morning, from my wages, and explained— Mrs. Price, how *did* you know about that?" In her amazement, Miss Chard forgot to look frightened. "Medora said she'd never tell a soul. But I suppose she forgot. Really, she was most understanding about it, Mrs. Price. Of course, I think her leniency was due wholly to her pleasure in discovering that the girl hadn't taken the money. Did she tell you everything, Mrs. Price?"

"No," Cassie said. "Uh—uh, no. Er—matter of fact, she never said anything to me about it."

"Then how do you know?"

"Oh, I don't!" Cassie said. "To be perfectly honest with you, I don't understand much more than you do. It's Bill." She indicated Leonidas. "He's the one who knows."

"He does? My, my," Miss Chard said, "I'm sure this is so confusing! But while I have the opportunity, Mr. Witherall, I must tell you how much I regret everything that happened this morning on the train. I've had no opportunity to tell you so before, everyone's been talking so quickly. I wrote you a little note, and mailed it this noon, so you'll get it to-morrow. But I *did* think you must be Leslie Horn's accomplice. Probably it was very stupid of me, but things were very confusing this morning. Very. And I didn't recognize you. I didn't know who you were till I looked in your wallet and saw your name. You're very different from that picture Medora has of you on her dresser."

"Wow!" Margie said softly.

Cassie giggled.

Leonidas ignored them both.

"D'you happen to know, Miss Chard, where Leslie Horn is now?"

Miss Chard made distressing little sounds, and clucked her tongue.

"Tch, tch, no! She got left behind on the Carnavon train, and Medora thinks she went back to New York. Well, really, I can't say that I blame her. Things must have been confusing for her, too, I'm sure. But Medora sent her a telegram, and just as soon as this robbery is settled, Medora intends to go right over and explain everything to her in person. I'd like to have the opportunity of explaining, myself," Miss Chard added, "but I've left Medora, so of course I can't go. But I intend to write her a little note. I should have, but—but it was rather hard to know just where to begin."

"M'yes, I can see where the beginning might have been difficult," Leonidas said. "What did Medora have to say at your leaving her service?"

"She said it was nonsense. Really," Miss Chard said, "I'm sure I don't know why I tell you these things. You can't possibly be interested."

"We're being awfully rude and curious, aren't we?" Cassie said quickly. "But you know me, and you see that Bill holds nothing against you for that crack on the head. And—please, just tell us things, Miss Chard. We'll explain it all later. It's important, believe me!"

"Yes, yes," Miss Chard said, "I supposed you must have some reason for being here. I expected that you'd be at the Voters League. That's such an important meeting. Perhaps you're going?"

"Perhaps. Er—tell me about this morning," Leonidas said. "You took Leslie's brush box, and her bill, and the gun and the handcuffs back to Dalton, and found the brush box was full of brushes, and the bill not one of those listed in your serial numbers. Then what took place?"

"Medora sent me to see if you'd got back. When you arrived, you frightened me," Miss Chard said, "rushing at me so, and I knew if you could run like that, you must be quite well again. When I got back to the house, I told Medora I was leaving her, and she said nonsense, we were going to the club. I told her I thought she should devote herself to the problem of who had stolen her money, and she said she knew. She said she was quite certain it hadn't been Leslie Horn, but she wished to make sure. So we took the bus to the lecture-luncheon. Really, I don't understand—"

"Please don't try to," Leonidas said. "Just tell me. With whom did she leave the lecture-luncheon?"

"Oh, I don't know. I tried so hard to find out, too. No one knew. Medora got up and said she saw Estelle Otis, and left me. And people were crowding around, and I lost sight of her completely."

"Estelle?" Cassie said blankly. "She left you to go see Estelle?"

"Yes. I think she's rather a dull woman, don't you?" Miss Chard said in an amazing burst of frankness. "But she's been around a lot lately, with the judge. That daughter really bores me."

"She bores everyone. Go on, Miss Chard," Cassie said. "You lost Medora. Then what?"

"I sat through the luncheon, and the lecture. I couldn't seem to see Medora anywhere. But it was all very confused, what with the lecturer being late, and people getting their cars stuck in the snow, and all that sort of thing. Later it was proposed that tea be held at Mr. Witherall's—"

"Who thought that up?" Cassie interrupted. "Was it Estelle?"

"I think she proposed it, yes. She and the judge. But I didn't feel it would be quite proper for me to attend, under the circumstances. And besides," Miss Chard said, "I told Medora that I was leaving her at once, and I wanted her to know that I meant it. So I took the bus to Florence Street. And what do you suppose? A man tried to steal my handbag! Really, this has been a most confusing day!"

"Wait till you hear our version," Cassie said. "By the way, how *is* your brother George?"

"Much better. The operation won't be necessary, after all. And the rector's found him a position as music director of the Carnavon Church. That was one of the reasons I came to the auditorium this evening. I knew the rector would be there, and I wished to thank him. Though, of course, I wrote him a little note. Really, there is quite a gathering at the auditorium. Your brother is there, Mrs. Price."

"Yeah," Cuff said. "The colonel's got on his best uniform, and all his medals and ribbons, and a man with more medals is with him. Margie says it's the dick from the train—"

"Indeed!" Leonidas said. "Indeed."

"Yeah. And Jock's there in his Scout uniform, with the Scout band. They're having a demonstration later, see? That's why my brothers was there. They was going to get four bits apiece for demonstrating, see? But I told 'em you'd make it up to 'em. This demonstration's going to be the biggest demonstration—"

"I haven't a doubt of it," Cassie said, "but don't let's hear another word about it for a few seconds, Cuff. Don't let's even wonder what Rutherford and Jock are doing there. Bill Shakespeare, if Medora went to see Estelle, and if Estelle— Oh, dear, Bill, this gets worse and worse! You'd better tell Miss Chard everything, quickly, right away!"

Leonidas drew a long breath.

When he finished speaking, Cassie looked at her watch.

"Five and a half minutes to put that in a nutshell," she said. "It's practically incredible. Miss Chard, we're awfully sorry. I know you and Medora have been together for so many years. But now you understand why we want to know things."

Miss Chard cleared her throat. She had made no comment during Leonidas's monologue, nor had her expression changed. Only once or twice she had shivered. But somehow, Cassie knew that the woman was ready to break down, and Leonidas guessed as much.

"I've always been afraid," Miss Chard fought the quiver in her voice, "that something like this might happen, Mrs. Price. I knew that harm would come of keeping money around. After all, even I succumbed and took some. And I told Medora yesterday that she should tell Colonel Carpenter everything. I said again this morning that he should be informed of everything. And, of course, I *did* call him. That is— well, Medora found that the money was missing around six o'clock yesterday, after the guests had gone. We had guests for tea."

"M'yes," Leonidas said. "That was the tea party planned for Leslie, was it not?"

Miss Chard nodded.

"Leslie told me she left a message about her departure, but we've never found it. The butler merely told us that Miss Horn had gone out, and we assumed that she'd gone for a walk."

"And you can find no trace of Leslie's note?" Leonidas said. "M'yes. Go on."

"It's that stupid butler," Cassie said.

"Thomas has been a thorn in my flesh for many years," Miss Chard said, "but it was not my place to question Medora's choice of servants. Then, Mrs. Price, we realized that Leslie Horn had really gone away. That she'd departed. And then we realized that the money was gone, too."

"And you called the colonel at that point?" Leonidas asked.

"Yes. And all those policemen came, with their guns. But before they arrived, Medora talked with Thomas, and decided that somehow or other there must have been a mistake, and that Leslie took the brush box off with her other artist's paraphernalia. When the colonel came, she told him that an error had been made, and that a friend had undoubtedly taken her box by mistake. Sometimes that safe door just opens of its own accord, and Medora wasn't at all sure that she'd put the box inside. She thought she might have left it out on the desk. The colonel was very solicitous, and said he hoped she was right, and that the money hadn't really been stolen. He was most kind."

"Didn't he suggest an investigation?" Leonidas inquired.

"Yes, but Medora refused. She said she'd settle things herself. Then she asked me to go to New York and get the girl. Under the circumstances, I was only too willing and eager to do so. If there were an official investigation—" Miss Chard left the sentence unfinished.

"M'yes," Leonidas said, "that would have been difficult for you. I fear that even the colonel would not have believed you. So you took a plane after Leslie."

"I went to the airport in a police car," Miss Chard said. "It was quite exciting, with the sirens. The colonel was very pleasant when Medora asked him if his men could give me a ride. He was always most tactful in his dealings with her."

"Rutherford's not dumb," Cassie said. "You can't ever tell when you'll need a pistol range. Bill, I begin to understand things. Rutherford was worried, and that's why he leapt on Margie— By the way, how did he work that? Did he give you a note to take to Medora?"

Margie nodded.

"He didn't explain anything to me, though, and I don't know what the note said. But that bunch of servants certainly put me to work! I never worked so hard in my life."

"Miss Chard," Leonidas said, "who came to tea yesterday afternoon?"

"About fifty. Quite a representative group. The rector, and Mrs. Tudbury, and Mrs. Otis, and many members of the Tuesday Club—you were asked, were you not, Mrs. Price?"

"Dear me, was I?" Cassie said. "That's probably one of those invitations that came while my bifocals were broken. Dear me! Bill Shakespeare, you know what I think? I think that someone at that tea party pinched Medora's money!"

"M'yes," Leonidas agreed absently. "Leslie's note,

too, I think. M'yes. Perhaps someone even saw Miss Chard take the hundred-dollar bill, and realized the splendid opportunity which presented itself. I concur, Cassie."

"Oh, no!" Miss Chard sounded shocked. "You're both wrong! It couldn't have been anyone at the party! Why, they were people we know! The better people. The nicer people. It wasn't any motley collection, like that group over at the auditorium— By the way, did you say you were going there?"

"Let's, Bill," Cuff said. "Let's go. The Voters League's going to announce their candidate for mayor, see, and it's going to be the biggest show they ever had in Dalton. Let's go, huh, Bill?"

"Cuff," Cassie said, "we're not going to that old auditorium to hear Scipione made candidate for mayor. Merciful heavens, with those two men in Bill's cellar, and not a whit of detecting done about Medora—with all that to settle, d'you think we can waste time going to monster demonstrations? Besides, I don't think it's going to be so monster. There wasn't much going on there when we circled around. Just some people with placards. Bill, now that you've found out how much money was stolen, what about it? What are you going to do? We've got to do something!"

Leonidas looked thoughtfully out the car windows at the bleak snow banks surrounding the Daltonham station.

The problem of what to do was bothering him intensely. He knew what he would like to do. How to do it was another thing.

"Well?" Cassie's foot was tapping the floor carpet. "What are you waiting for? The honking of geese?"

Leonidas watched a taxi swing up to the station door.

"Because," Cassie continued, "I think that action is indicated, Bill. It's high time. High time that— Bill! Where are you going?"

"Cuff," Leonidas opened the sedan's door, "come with me, please. Margie, keep Mrs. Price here. And Miss Chard, too. The geese have honked, Cassie. I'm about to act."

"Say, Bill," Cuff began eagerly, "you going after that little guy just got out of the cab, huh? That little guy?"

"Ssh! Yes! Come along!"

Obediently, Cuff followed Leonidas into the station.

"That little guy's in the Water Department, Bill," Cuff whispered in Leonidas's ear as they crossed the grimy waiting room. "I know him—"

"Ssh!"

Leonidas paused a few feet from the ticket window and listened as Ernest Round excitedly ordered a ticket to Milwaukee.

"A splendid city." Leonidas stepped forward and stood at Ernest Round's elbow. "A fine city. Er—distant."

"What?" Ernest swung around. "Oh. Oh, how do you do, Mr. Witherall. Fancy meeting you here!"

"M'yes," Leonidas said. "Fancy. We have your bag outside, Mr. Round. Let us take him to his bag, Cuff."

"Sure." Cuff took Ernest's other elbow.

Before Ernest was quite aware of what was happening to him, he had been gently propelled across the waiting room, out of the station, and into the sedan. His timid, hardly audible protests were utterly drowned out by Cuff's stalwart whistle.

"Do sit down beside Mrs. Price, Mr. Round," Leonidas said courteously. "Mr. Round was on the verge of going to Milwaukee, Cassie. D'you know Milwaukee well, Mr. Round?"

The judge, Leonidas thought, had trained the little man well. He answered obediently in spite of his complete bewilderment.

"No. Oh, no. I just got the telegram saying I was to come. This cousin of mine is ill. Henry Clay Round.

I haven't thought of him for years. They want me to come at once. I didn't think I ought to go, with the meeting at the auditorium, and all, but the judge insisted. She said it was my duty. It's pretty fine about my wife, isn't it?"

"You mean, her being the candidate for mayor? M'yes," Leonidas said. "M'yes indeed. It's very fine. Be still, Cassie."

"Er—I guess," Ernest squirmed on the back seat, "if you don't mind, I guess I'd better get on to Milwaukee. Did you say something about a bag outside?"

"Very possibly," Leonidas swung his pince-nez, "I did mention a bag. Persiflage, entirely. Mr. Round, I wish you'd relax and tell me when this telegram arrived from Henry Clay."

"This evening. Just after we got back from your house. After helping Elsa with the Pussycats. Really, I feel I should be going. Really. I'm late now. The judge needed our car, so she asked some friends of hers to come and take me to the station—she had to be getting on to the auditorium, of course. But they didn't come, and I had to take a taxicab—"

Leonidas pushed Mr. Round gently back against the seat.

"M'yes. Friends of the judge. Could one possibly have been Lieutenant Rossi?"

"Yes. But he didn't come. I suppose he was too busy. He's very active with the Voters League. I said I thought it was asking too much of him, but the judge said he would be glad to give me a ride."

"Wow!" Margie said. "Wow! Another ride. Bill, they got the jitters. They're scared. Another ride!"

"Just one ride," Ernest Round said. "Just here to the station."

"Bill," Cassie spoke in a voice of ominous calm, "those placards said 'Round for Mayor!' I thought they said 'Hound the Mayor!'"

"It was 'Round for Mayor,'" Ernest said proudly. "It sounds well, don't you think? You know, I hoped I might be mayor, myself, when I started in the Water Department. That was thirty-seven years ago next week. But of course things are different now. It's pretty complicated to be mayor, these days. Hustle, and bustle, and excitement. I really hate to go off to Milwaukee and miss the best part, tonight at the auditorium. But, as Hattie said, I did my part, saving those papers yesterday."

"Ah," Leonidas said. "Those papers you took from the tea party, perhaps? Er—were you at the tea party?"

"He was there," Miss Chard said. "Medora definitely remembered him when we were trying to think if any outsiders had come to the house. He got some papers from the judge, and rushed off. But I thought I saw your car later, out by the corner, Mr. Round?"

"Yes, Dow hailed me as I went by," Mr. Round said. "I was in a tremendous hurry, because the judge wanted the papers put in her office safe at once. They were trying to blackmail her, you know, but she got the papers. And then Dow hailed me and asked me about the water connection—really, that's a very interesting installation Dow has there. Very. I've enjoyed watching that installation, Mr. Wither-all. I might say it's been an eye-opener, as I tried to tell the judge when I tried to explain to her. You see, ordinarily the main conduit—"

"M'yes, quite," Leonidas said. "Dow hailed you, and you went into my house to view my interesting connections. Did you take the papers with you?"

Ernest Round sighed.

"As I told the judge, it seemed like the best idea. I suppose I should have done as she told me, and taken the papers straight to her office. I shouldn't have stopped. But that main hookup was so very interesting, and I didn't think it would matter if I stopped for a few minutes. So I took the box of papers in with me. And then, while I was in the kitchen, I heard Colonel Carpenter talking on the phone—"

"Rutherford!" Cassie said. "He's been in on this all the time! Go on, Ernest. Quick!"

"Well," Ernest said unhappily, "I don't know who the colonel was talking to, or what about, but he very distinctly said, 'I know who has the papers, and I'll get them at once.' And—well, I had a moment of panic. I remembered how important Hattie said those papers I had were. And—well—"

"You opened my red refrigerator," Leonidas said, "and put the papers inside. Isn't that so?"

"That's it," Ernest said. "So it was you who found the papers and gave them back to Hattie! You see, I realized almost at once that the colonel wasn't referring to my papers, but when I opened the refrigerator, they were gone. Disappeared. Hattie couldn't understand that, but it's just what happened. There was a click, and they disappeared. Hattie just wouldn't believe it, but that's what happened."

"I bet," Cassie said, "that the judge was pretty perturbed, wasn't she, when you broke the news?"

Ernest sighed again.

"I don't think I've ever seen her so upset! She told Lieutenant Rossi, and he was terribly upset, too. But later last night, Hattie said everything was all right, and for me to forget the whole thing. So I did. You know what I'm afraid? I'm afraid I've missed my train to Milwaukee!"

"Mr. Round," Leonidas said, "I have a splendid idea. Why don't you take a plane? Then you could go to the auditorium, and then Cuff will drive you into Boston, and you can get a plane."

"The judge wouldn't approve," Ernest said at once. "She wouldn't think it safe." He hesitated. "On the other hand, I do want to be at the auditorium, so much!"

"We'll make all the arrangements," Leonidas said. "Cuff, take Mr. Round into the station, and get his luggage, and then bring him back to the car. Er— take your time."

"Bill," Cassie said, as Cuff and Ernest left, "d'you mean—Bill, d'you feel sure about all this?"

"The Voters League, Cassie, has political power. But the Voters League needs money. If you had political aspirations, and money, it's quite possible that you might make a deal with the Voters League. And to be Mayor of Dalton is, as Dow assured me, definitely a step up. Medora had cash. And the judge took it. You fit the judge in, Cassie, and you'll find she works out. She's hidden behind Estelle's skirts sometimes, but she's there."

"Poor Ernest!" Cassie said. "Poor little man. Just a tool. And she was going to let Rossi take him for a ride! And he's so proud of a Round being mayor! But, Bill, you're still stymied! You know what Rutherford thinks of circumstantial evidence. You'll never be able to prove any of this in fifty million years. Never. At nine-thirty, in fifteen minutes—didn't you tell me nine-thirty, Margie? Well, at nine-thirty, she's going to be made candidate for mayor, with acclaim. And what Rossi'll do—"

"Fifteen minutes," Leonidas said. "So. Cassie, how many people would you need to start a good, acclaiming demonstration?"

Cassie looked at him thoughtfully.

"Well, I'm pretty good by myself, Bill. And there's Margie. And Cuff. Mrs. Pankhurst always used to say that three was the ideal number to start things."

"Were you a suffragette?" Miss Chard leaned forward. "Really? So was I. I was in charge of a brigade, you know, in England. I'm quite good at demonstrations."

"Why, Miss Chard, you old sport!" Cassie said happily. "Bill, just what do you want done in the line of a demonstration? I do hope it's what I think!"

"Listen," Leonidas said. "Listen carefully, Margie, because you'll have to translate to Cuff. I want to get things straightened out before he returns with Ernest. Now, Cassie, you and Miss Chard—"

Ten minutes later, Cuff drew the sedan up in front of the thronged auditorium steps. A harassed-looking policeman yelled at them to move on, and then, catching sight of Cassie, smiled broadly and indicated with a gesture that they could park anywhere as long as they liked.

"Isn't that nice!" Cassie said. "It's Anderson. He'll do anything I say. Margie, you and Cuff get the Ward Four boys. Oh, Anderson! Help me through the crowd, will you?"

"Hi, Mrs. Price," Anderson said. "I been wondering why you wasn't here to see the fun."

"Oh, Anderson," Cassie said, "I'm supposed to be sitting up on the platform in my best dress, and I got delayed— Can you shove us through this mob?"

"Wait'll I get Feeny and Slim," Anderson said. "Then you can get behind us, and we'll have you on that platform in no time. Say, I seen Jock inside."

"I want him," Cassie said. "Thank you, Anderson. Isn't this marvelous, Miss Chard! A flying wedge!"

"What do you think of this Round for Mayor business?" Anderson had to yell to make himself heard.

"Marvelous!" Cassie yelled back. "He's with us, you know. Mr. Witherall's got him—"

"*Him?*"

"He's with Mr. Witherall. We had an accident, and that's why we're so late. His car got stuck—"

"Him? You mean *her!*"

Cassie laughed merrily.

"*Him*, Anderson. You've been listening to that propaganda. Wait, there's Jock. Jock, come here! And bring that boy with the bugle. Chard, you start down that aisle. Bill, you and Ernest wait for Cuff's boys—what did you say, Ernest?"

Ernest cupped his hands to his mouth.

"I said, Mrs. Price, are we late for the demonstration?"

Cassie smiled.

"We're just in time to start it. Jock, lift that placard. Tell that boy to blow something. Reveille will do. Now!"

Fifteen minutes later, to his intense surprise, Ernest Round had been acclaimed the Voters League candidate for the Mayor of Dalton. The Ward Four demonstrators, delighted to find that Round was a man after all, were vociferous in their joy. They didn't, as Cuff found time to tell Leonidas, like the idea of a lady mayor, anyway, not even at four bits a head. A man was better.

The Tuesday Club, after the first startled gasp, rallied loyally. It was, as Mrs. Tudbury said, all in the family.

Leonidas, with Miss Chard and Cassie and Jock grouped around him, surveyed the bedlam from the rear of the auditorium.

"There," he said, "is as fine and spontaneous a demonstration as was ever inspired. Let us leave it, before my eardrums split."

Cassie coughed as they walked down the deserted front steps of the building.

"Chard," she said hoarsely, "you were marvelous. I think we should feel proud!"

Miss Chard coughed.

"I think so," she said with pride. "Of course, I'm a little out of practice, but I think that went off quite well."

"Jock, your friends were marvelous, too," Cassie said. "That boy with the bugle must go to a matinee with us. I think I can truthfully say that not even Ernest Round is sure how that happened, and no one will ever know. No one will dare say a word, or question things, after that din. They can't claim that was a mistake. They'd never dare. Did they get the judge out to the car? That shoulder-lifting was a stroke of pure genius, Bill."

"Why, those friends of Cuff's," Jock said, "they just lifted the judge off that platform before she knew what was happening to her. And the way they whisked her out the side door! And was she ever mad! She was purple!"

"She was frothing," Cassie said, "but there wasn't a single thing she could do but let herself be carried out on their shoulders. Cuff had her in a viselike grip. My, aren't things like that catching? I saw people carting Mrs. Tudbury around!"

"And the rector, too," Miss Chard said. "The choir had him. Did the colonel follow Judge Round out? Did that part work out?"

"Oh, yes," Jock said. "I made straight for Uncle Root and told him, and he followed them out. They got into a sedan out front. Uncle, and Cuff and Margie, and the judge, and that friend of uncle's, and some of Cuff's friends. They'll be at your house, Bill, by now. You know how Cuff drives." He paused and cleared his throat. "Gran, I think Uncle Root knows quite a lot."

"Practically all," Cassie said. "I only hope he won't be too angry with us— Hail that cab, Bill. I'm too exhausted to think of getting Simeon from the parking lot."

Dow and Leslie met the group at the door of Forty Birch Hill Road.

"Come in," Dow said. "We've just heard about the Round family— Somehow, after what we've been through today, it doesn't even amaze me. Cassie, I'm momentarily disengaged! Elsa dropped in with those kids on their way home, just after the Camera Club left. By the way, the locksmith's coming to change the locks. I phoned him. Anyway, Elsa came, and I had a brain wave, and told her I was going to build us a little nest like this place, and she busted the engagement. Leslie's still being coy, but she's agreed to come home and meet mother—"

"Stop gabbling," Cassie said. "Where's Rutherford, and everyone?"

"Downstairs," Dow said. "Judge Harriet Pomeroy Round is in a stew."

"Did she confess?" Miss Chard asked eagerly.

"Everything," Dow said. "The colonel sold her the idea that it was a bona fide, genuine double-cross that Ernest pulled on her, and Hattie boiled over and told all—"

"Hah!" the tall, erect figure of Colonel Carpenter loomed in the hallway. "Hah! You!"

"Now don't *boom* at us!" Cassie said anxiously. "There isn't any need to boom! Did she tell everything?"

"Hah!" the colonel said. "Yes. Have to sort out the facts from what she thinks of Ernest, though. She wants to kill him, now. Claimed first that no one had any proof. I fooled her. Saw her this noon in a car with Medora. Know how she got Medora here? Just said, 'Come along and I'll give you back the money.' Pretended to be conscience-stricken. Said 'Come.' And Medora was fool enough to come. Walked right into it. Spider and fly."

"Who's the man that came on the train?" Cassie asked.

"Kern. He saw Medora and Hattie together in the car, too. Kern's the feller I sent for to take a look at Rossi. Have a nice trip, Bill, hah?"

"Dull," Leonidas said. "Is Rossi the one that Kern wanted?"

"Wants him," the colonel said with satisfaction, "for every damn count on the books. I was waiting to see what this League thing would bring forth. Knew something was up. Hattie says she's going to appeal to the highest court in the land. If you ask me, she'll get to a psychopathic ward before she gets to any court. That's the trouble with women in politics. Don't know when to stop." He glared at Cassie. "Lucky thing Jock didn't come here early."

"Oh, Rutherford, you're *not* going to be cross at us!" Cassie said.

"I saw Jock get on that pung," the colonel said. "Saw him myself. I told him never to. Too dangerous. So when I saw him, I followed him up here to make sure he was safe. I dropped past later, and there's Dow driving off with Jock in a bundle. Disgraceful. Lucky thing you never opened that door. Hindering justice. Know the penalty, hah?"

"Where's the money, darling?" Cassie said. "Have you found it?"

"Thought Bill would know," the colonel said. "Do you, Bill?"

Leonidas led them into the kitchen and opened the door of the red refrigerator.

"Hah," the colonel said. "That's not like my icebox. My light's on the side. Very nice, though. What of it?"

"Mr. Round," Leonidas said, "nervously put a brush box, which he thought contained important papers, in this icebox yesterday afternoon. He said there was a click, and when he opened the door, the papers were gone. Watch, now."

"Hah!" the colonel said. "I see! The light pops out of that screened place when you open the door. Slips back when you shut it. Brush box went down there, hah? How'd you guess?"

"The celery heart I put in this morning," Leonidas said, "was not there when we removed the contents of the icebox this afternoon. I'd put it up top, by the light. So—"

"You guessed all the time!" Cassie said. "Why didn't you tell us?"

"I thought," Leonidas said, "since no one else guessed, I might as well not make the fact public— Jock, will you get a screw driver? You see, colonel, first they tried to get the refrigerator. Then they hoped that Tudbury's Horse would bring things to light. Then, of course, we'd be taken away for questioning, and leave them a clear field. All they had to do was to come and get the money at their leisure. Then they tried to frighten us away. Tell me, Miss Chard, was the judge late for the lecture-luncheon?"

"Oh, very late! Her car was stuck, she said."

"M'yes," Leonidas said. "What a satisfactory thing a snowstorm is. Er—have you got it, colonel?"

"Got the celery," the colonel said. "The damn brush box is stuck. Get Cuff, Jock. He's downstairs, hurling epithets at Rossi."

Between them, the colonel and Cuff finally fished out the brush box from the opening where the little floodlight slid back.

"Hah," the colonel said. "He pushed it in, and it popped down, when he closed the door. Look out for your fingernail, Jock. Money inside the box, is it? Good. Know the trouble, Bill, why they didn't get that last night? I was here till two, fixing the tools. Told the prowl-car men to stay here—terrible night, you know. Terrible storm. Had calls switched to your phone. They didn't leave till six, after the street was plowed."

"And my Italians came to shovel at six," Cassie said. "I phoned 'em last night. And then after they left, Car Fifteen was on the corner. And then Bill came. Rutherford, will you make him a sergeant?"

"Why, for God's sakes?" Colonel Carpenter forgot to boom. "Bill doesn't want to be a sergeant! Do you, Bill?"

"Cuff! I mean Cuff, you big goon! Won't you make him a sergeant?"

"Hah," the colonel said. "Suppose so, if you teach him the answers. No telling what he'll do if he doesn't get enough money to marry that girl. Take away the whole damn golf course! Cass, I've got to see to Hattie. Kern's watching her while she and Rossi are doing a little paper work. Confessions, hah! Want some eggs when I'm through."

He paused in the doorway.

"Heard from Muir today," he said. "Muir's coming back next week. With Rossi out of the way, I'm going to hand things over to Muir. Take a trip. S'pose you're settling down, hah, Bill?"

"Of course he is!" Cassie said. "And I don't think you ought to consider any trips, Rutherford. It's dangerous. Wars, bombings, all sorts of things!"

"Er—in two weeks," Leonidas said. "M'yes. Two weeks will be enough."

Two weeks, Leonidas reflected, were always enough in which to tear off a Lieutenant Haseltine story.

"Right," the colonel said briskly. "Two weeks. Round the world again, hah?"

"Fine," Leonidas said. "Splendid."

"The two of you are crazy!" Cassie said. "You can't be so foolish! Why, it's dangerous! Wars, and bombings, and more wars, and more bombings! You simply can't go around the world! You stay right here in Dalton, where it's safe, and—and quiet—and—and restful."

Leonidas bit his lip.

"Like today?"

"Well," Cassie said, "well—oh, dear! I can't say a thing. What's two weeks enough for?"

Leonidas smiled, and swung his pince-nez.

"The tentative title, as suggested by my dear friend the Maharajah," he said, "is Cold Steal."